SEND NO BLESSINGS

Beth heard her father's voice through the bedroom wall: ". . . was talking to George at the diner yesterday. Told him my oldest girl's turning sixteen in the spring. He says bring her by after her birthday and he'll give her a try as a waitress. Full-time. Minimum wage to start and raises regular if she measures up. . . ."

Beth felt as though her lungs had frozen. For a moment a panicky feeling welled up inside her as she struggled for breath. She waited numbly for her mother's reply.

The bed creaked again. Another sigh. "Don't know as she'd put her heart in it," Lorna said at last.

"Don't have to put her heart into it. Put her back to it, like you and me been doing all our lives. Elizabeth thinks she's too good for waitress work, she's got another think coming."

Beth's arms fell limply to her sides, her heart pounding. . . .

I'm not leaving school when I'm sixteen, she said, making no sound, but forming the words with her lips. She took her pencil and engraved the word *not* on the cover of her notebook, the lead going clear through the cardboard.

You saying no to me, girl? her father would ask if she told him.

And somehow she'd have to get up the courage to say yes.

SEND NO BLESSINGS

Phyllis Reynolds Naylor

A Jean Karl Book

Puffin Books

This work was supported by a grant from the National Endowment for the Arts.

PUFFIN BOOKS
Published by the Penguin Group
Viking Penguin, a division of Penguin Books USA Inc.,
375 Hudson Street, New York, New York 10014, U.S.A.
Penguin Books Ltd, 27 Wrights Lane, London W8 5TZ, England
Penguin Books Australia Ltd, Ringwood, Victoria, Australia
Penguin Books Canada Ltd, 10 Alcorn Avenue, Toronto, Ontario, Canada M4V 3B2
Penguin Books (N.Z.) Ltd, 182–190 Wairau Road, Auckland 10, New Zealand
Penguin Books Ltd, Registered Offices: Harmondsworth, Middlesex, England

First published in the United States of America by Atheneum,
an imprint of Macmillan Publishing Company, 1990
Published in Puffin Books, 1992
5 7 9 10 8 6
Copyright © Phyllis Reynolds Naylor, 1990
All rights reserved

LIBRARY OF CONGRESS CATALOGING-IN-PUBLICATION DATA
Naylor, Phyllis Reynolds.
Send no blessings / by Phyllis Reynolds Naylor.   p.   cm.
"First published in the United States of America by Atheneum
. . . 1990"—T.p. verso.
Summary: A teenager in a large family that lives in a trailer
yearns for love, approval, an escape from endless chores, and a
chance to make something of herself; when a good and decent man,
seven years her senior, falls in love with her, she realizes
marriage to him could solve her problems.
ISBN 0-14-034859-X (pbk.)
[1. Family life—Fiction.   2. West Virginia—Fiction.]   I. Title.
[PZ7.N24Se 1992]   [Fic]—dc20   91-31813

Printed in the United States of America
Set in Stempel Garamond

To Doris Lynch,
for her wise counsel and friendship,
and to my aunt, Eileen Schield,
my patron saint in Iowa

SEND NO
BLESSINGS

1

It was when the yellow bus crossed the bridge and turned right that Beth always wished she were invisible. Like the story she once heard of a bus driver over in Mingo County who claimed that on his last run of the evening, as he passed the cemetery, someone always pulled the cord to get off. Except that the bus was empty. Every night when the bus passed the cemetery, the bell would ding, the driver would stop, he'd open the doors, but no one was there.

Beth would have liked that now—would have liked, when the school bus reached her home—to slip off as quietly and invisibly as that ghost in Mingo County, so that when people asked, "Who lives there?" no one would answer.

The bus lurched and made the turn, gears grinding as the driver shifted down to second, then to third again. The New River, to the right of the roadway, was low. The weather had been dry that autumn, and now the river revealed its secrets, from small stepping-stones to great boulders—dozens of them—sunning themselves, bleaching dry white in the warmth of the October afternoon.

"We going to live by the *river*?" Beth had squealed when she was five, sitting in her father's lap as he steered—Mother, Geraldine, and Lyle crowded in beside them on moving day.

Beth smiled wryly to herself. You could tell a five-year-old she was going to live in a box, and as long as she had her family with her, she wouldn't care.

On either side of the river the hills rose high and steep—behind the town of Crandall on the opposite bank and just off the roadway on the side where the bus was moving now. Only a week ago the hills had been spectacular, as though a huge patchwork quilt had been thrown over the West Virginia mountains. Beth had sat on a rock by the river and tried to count the different shades of red and gold, interspersed here and there with the dark, rich color of evergreens. Now the trees were mostly bare, but the red-tipped twigs of the sour-woods and maples gave the hills a lavender, feathery look. Beautiful land, beautiful trees, beautiful river, beautiful sky, and then there was the Herndons' trailer home, like a sore on the face of God.

"Sure is a pretty day," the bus driver said to no one in particular, but Beth, sitting in the front row, knew that it was directed at her. Mrs. Shayhan, the driver, in her brown vinyl jacket, made a point of saying a little something to all the students as they got on or off the bus. Beth hoped that if she didn't answer, Mrs. Shayhan would let it drop—not say anything else to call attention to Beth or the fact that they were reaching her home. But the silence seemed rude somehow, and so, as the bus slowed and the big red STOP sign by the driver's window flipped out, Beth said:

"You've got a line of cars behind us. After I get out, you go on ahead."

Mrs. Shayhan swung the lever and the door opened: "Not a one of those folks in a bigger hurry than we are. You cross on over first, Beth. It's the law."

The conversation on the bus died out momentarily as it always seemed to do when the bus reached the Herndons' stop. In less than a second Beth had slipped out the door (she never stood up until the doors were open and her escape was clear) and then walked quickly across the road, head down.

If you happened to be looking up, when the bus stopped, at the high, rocky wall on the left, you would wonder where somebody could live on this part of the road—river to one side, rock the other. But then, as your eye moved down, you'd see that the cliff swerved in just a little for thirty yards or so, and in this small half-moon of land off the roadway, someone had put a house trailer, double-wide. There was a smaller trailer squeezed in beside it; they met each other in a sort of V, both of them hooked up with the electric lines that followed the road.

Last month, when Beth had started tenth grade and got on the bus for the first time, she had walked the full length of the aisle to the stares of the other students, and that same afternoon, when she got off the bus again, half sentences had followed her out the door: "Fish camp?" ". . . a mess of children . . ." "*Eight* kids?"

From that day on, Beth always sat at the front of the bus, always slipped out as quickly as she could when it stopped, always shut her ears to what the others might be saying.

Now, as she transferred her books to her other arm and the bus went on, she saw something move across the narrow space between the trailers and disappear. Beth crouched down and looked beneath. Two small legs were creeping around the Maxwells' trailer. Grinning, Beth edged over to the corner and, the moment the first blond curl appeared, grabbed her young sister with a loud "Got'cha!" Shirley split the air with her shriek.

"Acker backer, sodie cracker—can't catch me!" four-year-old Shirley taunted, squirming loose and running off again. Beth gave chase, then changed directions, colliding with Shirley behind the trailers, then chasing her out toward the front again.

This time Beth let her go, leaning against the one frail tree that grew beside the rocky cliff, and stared at her family's trailer. The first time she'd done this, standing out by the road long after the high-school bus had gone and looking at her home with new eyes, she had felt her face turning the color of sumac. When she was in junior high, she'd always gotten off with a friend in the trailer court down the road, then walked the rest of the way later. But now the friend had moved away and Mrs. Shayhan must have thought she was doing Beth a favor by letting her out right across from her home.

Why, Beth had wondered ever since, had her eyes never focused on the Crisco can holding up one corner of the dilapidated porch her father had built, or the old refrigerator standing outside in the rain? The torn sheets of plastic over the windows or, at the base of the cliff, the pile of junk that seemed to grow higher and wider with each passing year and was never carted away?

It was then, just six weeks ago, that she had begun to see what she had kept hidden even from herself, to hear what she had tuned out before, to feel the kinds of things that made her silent now around the house. Her own little world at the foot of the cliff had developed a crack, and others were looking in.

"Elizabeth Pearl?"

From another room, her mother's voice sailed in high and sharp above the whine of Douglas, the youngest of the Herndon children.

"Yes, ma'am?"

Mrs. Herndon came out of a back bedroom carrying a bundle of laundry and fending off three-year-old Douglas, who was pestering her arm. "You and Shirley out there screamin' like savages, and you the oldest of the lot."

"Shirley was about to catch me," Beth joked, reaching for the Ritz crackers, and Shirley, who had followed her in, giggled.

"You're still one big child, I swear to God. But don't you never lose your squeal."

"My what?" Beth stuck a cracker in her mouth and turned.

Mrs. Herndon smiled. "Your squeal. That's what your daddy used to call it. All you kids, when you was little, finding delight in the smallest thing. You was the worst, though. You see something for the first time and you start to crow like it was you who invented it. I remember once you found a tiny hole in the sidewalk, and there was a flower growing out of it. Think it was just a dandelion, but how you squealed and carried on. And Ray says, 'Hope she don't never lose her squeal.' "

"I never heard him say that."

"He can't hardly get a word in edgewise now, that's why, all these kids around."

Shirley was reaching for a cracker, but Beth held the box above her head. "Say please," she instructed.

"Please," the child said.

"Pretty please."

"*Pretty* please."

Beth grinned. "Pretty please with molasses and brown sugar on it."

"Pretty please m'lasses . . ."

Laughing, Beth sat down and hauled the girl onto her lap, giving her the cracker. Shirley leaned back against her, chewing contentedly, legs dangling on either side.

"I eat all day and don't gain an ounce," Beth complained.

"You got my bones, that's why." Mrs. Herndon slid onto the vinyl dinette seat across from her, also taking a cracker. "Don't know that I even stopped for lunch today. I eat like a movie star, how come I don't look like a movie star?"

"All you need is some of that forty-dollar-a-bottle makeup," Beth teased.

"That and new hair, new teeth . . ."

6

"You've got pretty hair, Ma."

Lorna Herndon sighed. "Mrs. Goff wants six dozen more daisies and two or three dozen of them little blue violets. Wanted to know could she have them tomorrow and I said it was likely."

"Why doesn't she give us more notice, Ma? She think we're just sitting here waiting to make flowers? I've got a biology test tomorrow!"

"Well, which is going to do us more good? Now answer me that." A trace of sharpness returned to her mother's voice, but then she softened. "You do what you can. I've got the washing tonight, but I'll work on them flowers some afterwards."

Douglas was running around in circles now, wearing only a little striped polo shirt, his legs and bottom bare. The house smelled of dirty pants.

Mrs. Herndon surveyed him wearily. "I told him he mess himself one more time he can go with*out* pants, and he don't even care."

"You've got to praise him when he does right."

"Seven children I train up as quick as you please and the eighth got all the mischief. . . ."

Beth turned the box of crackers over to Shirley and went back into the main room. One side of the trailer was almost a duplicate of the other—two small bedrooms, one bath, a main room where the two halves of the double-wide trailer were joined, and a kitchen that also extended from one side to the other.

There was a card table in the corner, covered with little

boxes, each filled with plastic flower parts. Sitting down in the folding chair with NEVILLE FUNERAL HOME stenciled on its back, Beth reached into one box for a short length of wire, into another for a long coil of green tape, and into a third for three artificial leaves. Deftly her fingers held the tape at the bottom of the wire and began to wind, as Mrs. Goff had taught her, anchoring the leaves at intervals until she was ready to insert the daisy at the top. First the round yellow center, which she impaled at the end of the wire, then the white petals, one at a time, pushing their sharp ends into the spongy center, securing them fast. One flower done . . . two . . . three . . . her fingers almost a blur as she worked.

They were paid by the dozen, Beth and her mother. When they sat at the card table together and worked, they looked almost like sisters, their long, straight, walnut-brown hair reaching their shoulders, Mother's streaked with gray; gray-green eyes, cheekbones high as a crow's nest, lips not any thicker than a shoelace. Where Beth's skin was smooth as a china plate, however, Mother's was beginning to crinkle about the eyes, but she was still pretty.

At Goffs' Motel, where Mother did cleaning, Marjorie Goff sold flower arrangements that she displayed on the shelf behind the cash register in the restaurant. Every few weeks she ordered more flowers. Of the money earned, Beth was allowed to keep half.

"You got fingers like wings," Lorna had told her once, and the praise itself almost lifted Beth from the chair and sailed her around the room, she got so little of it.

It was true that she was fast. Doing things with her hands

8

came easy for Elizabeth Pearl Herndon. English and biology did not, but typing was like she'd been born with her fingers to the keys. Only six weeks into the course, and Beth was already the fastest in the class.

A second school bus ground to a stop out on the road. Douglas ran to the door and pushed open the screen.

"Douglas, you get yourself back in here!" Beth yelled.

Little Shirley shrieked with merriment and only pretended to hold him back. She let go of his shirt and shrieked again as Douglas ran out on the porch and down the steps.

Beth gave a disgusted smile and got up to retrieve him, but the next-youngest children were coming home on the elementary-school bus and were already crossing the road.

Bud and Betty Jo, seven and nine, burst through the door, laughing at Douglas without his pants, but ten-year-old Ruth Marie was furious and came in scowling, Douglas squirming in her arms.

"Ma!" she yelled, dropping him. "Douglas was outside naked and all the kids *saw*!"

"Well, maybe that'll put some shame in him then," Mother called from the kitchen. "He don't look out, he'll still be messing himself in kindergarten."

One more year, Beth told herself, and surely Douglas would be toilet trained. No more smell of diapers around the house. Two more years, and all eight children would be in school. Mother wouldn't have to pay Mrs. Maxwell to watch Douglas and Shirley while she cleaned rooms at Goffs', and when Father had his Wednesdays off as grill man for the diner over in Crandall, he wouldn't have to listen to a "mess of magpies," as he called his brood. Things would settle down. *If* there were no more babies. . . .

Beth reached for another wire, another leaf. Three more years, and she would have graduated. Then what? The Big Question. She did not picture herself in this trailer house forever. Where, then? She wasn't sure. But she did know, as truly as there was sassafras in West Virginia, that her parents expected her to live at home until she married. It wasn't something they talked about much, but whenever Beth got even near the subject, her parents never acknowledged that there were choices. Didn't even see, it seemed, the restlessness growing inside her.

Ruth Marie was still indignant. She dropped her books on the floor and glared around the room. "My friends probably think Douglas doesn't even *own* any pants, the way he runs around."

"A lot of kids have baby brothers," Beth told her, rhythmically sticking on the petals of still another flower.

"Not running around naked, they don't. I was never so embarrassed in my life."

"That's the most embarrassing thing ever happen to you, you got a fine life ahead," said their mother. "Now pick them books up before I fall over 'em, break my neck."

Beth herself had helped raise some of the children. When she was only five years old, in fact, she had held Ruth Marie for her mother and given her a bottle. She had done the same for Betty Jo. By the time Bud had come along, then Shirley and Douglas, Beth was changing diapers, spooning cereal into mouths, bathing babies. . . . Half her life—*more* than half her life—had been taken up with babies, and she was only fifteen.

She realized suddenly that she was working in shadow and reached over to turn on the lamp. One minute it was broad afternoon and the next the sun had gone over the rim of the mountain, leaving the air colder, the sky dim. When you lived in hill country, it took a while for the sun to get going in the morning, and just about the time you'd begun to warm your bones, the sun was gone again, and the gaps and hollows had become canyons once more.

The pile of daisies grew higher. Beth heard Dad's pickup coming the same time the third bus arrived, this one from the junior high school, and the last contingent of Herndons was home. Geraldine came in, holding her radio to her ear; then Lyle, heading for the refrigerator. A few minutes later Dad walked through the door and hung up his jacket. The main room was noisy now, crowded, the TV blaring. It seemed to Beth as though every square inch of the double-wide trailer was spoken for, and you didn't hardly turn around to escape one pair of eyes looking at you, you were facing another.

Ray Herndon got a soft drink from the kitchen, grabbed at Douglas as he barreled by, tickling his stomach, then came out and stood beside the card table. He was a small man, wiry as the stems Beth held in her fingers.

Beth liked to be watched while she worked, the way her fingers flew. The daisies hung over the side of the table now, she'd done so many. She smiled up at her father.

"Petals are crooked," he said, taking another swallow of Sprite.

"They don't have to be straight, Dad, as long as they're hooked in good. Makes them look more real." She held one out in front of her dramatically. "Fresh from the field and wet with dew!"

"You wind them leaves in good now," her father said. "Don't want 'em falling off."

"My leaves don't ever fall off," she told him, then sighed. "I got six dozen of these to do and some violets. Violets are the hardest."

"Well, you don't finish you can always stay home tomorrow and work on them. Get yourself ahead some."

"I'm not staying home from school, Dad! I've got a biology test!"

"You saying no to me, girl?"

Beth glanced up at him, lips apart. His eyes, blue as sky and cold as glass, stared back.

"I'll finish them tonight," she said in answer.

Ray Herndon walked over to the window, looking out at the river, and Beth studied his back. This was the man who had wanted her to keep her "squeal"? The father who used to let her sit in his lap when he drove the truck, who had made a popgun for her once out of elder wood and hickory? It seemed to Beth he was often mad at her lately, but for the life of her she couldn't remember what she'd said or done.

When supper was ready, Beth cleared off the card table. The three youngest children ate on the sofa, their plates in their laps, and the others divided themselves between the dinette in the kitchen and the card table in the main room.

Betty Jo finished first and made a dessert by sugaring her

buttered bread. "We going out trick-or-treating this year, Dad?" she asked, swinging her legs back and forth under her chair.

"You behave yourself, I reckon somebody will take you." He smiled at her. "What you going to be?"

She shrugged.

"Look," said twelve-year-old Lyle, and everyone turned in his direction. He had taken the dark red skin of a bean from his plate and pressed it against one tooth. When he smiled he appeared to have an open space between his teeth. The family laughed. "I'm going as a tramp," he said. "Rub coal on my cheeks for whiskers."

"Can we go even if it rains?" Ruth Marie asked, as if trying to extract a promise, and Beth remembered the year before when it had poured buckets. They'd started out in the pickup, three children squeezed in beside their father, four more riding in the open back, and had had to go home after only two or three stops, the children drenched.

"You're asking me to know the weather a week from today and I don't even know will it rain tomorrow," Ray Herndon said, and got up to help himself to more ham and beans from the stove.

Mother drove the truck to the Laundromat that evening, and it was long after ten when she got back. Beth was still making violets, working by the light of a small lamp so as not to disturb Lyle, who slept on the couch.

"Go on to bed," Mother told her. "I'll finish the rest."

"You sure?"

"You got a test tomorrow, I reckon you can use the sleep."

Beth took a flashlight to get into bed without stubbing her toe. Hers was the smallest of the two tiny bedrooms in this section of the trailer, and there was scarcely room for the double bed she shared with Geraldine. Still holding the flashlight, Beth propped her pillow against the wall and opened her biology notebook.

She shone the light on the pages, turning softly. If Dad knew she was in here studying—that Mother was doing the flowers alone . . .

Thirteen-year-old Geraldine stirred, rolled halfway over, and squinted, her yellow-brown hair hanging down over her eyes. "What are you *doing*?"

"Just lay back down and don't tell, either," Beth whispered. "I got a test tomorrow and I'm already fighting a *D*."

"What's it on?" Geraldine asked sleepily.

"Frogs."

"Sweet Jesus!" The way those words came out of Mother's mouth when she said them, they were a prayer. The way they came out of Geraldine's, they weren't.

Closing the book at last, Beth concentrated on the Xeroxed handout of a frog's anatomy that the teacher had given her, all the parts labeled for memorizing: *the dorsal and ventral roots of the spinal nerves; the pectoralis muscle, the maxillary bone, the mandibular arch* . . .

Gradually Geraldine's arm slipped off the side of her face until at last it fell limp onto the sheet. She gave a grunt and rolled over again, away from the beam of the flashlight.

Beth studied until she could name all the frog's parts with the answers covered. There were still some general questions on amphibians to look over, but she could review those at breakfast.

On the other side of the wall, her mother was getting ready for bed. Dad usually went first because he had to be at the diner at seven in the morning, but he often couldn't sleep until Mother came.

It was embarrassing sometimes—the noises. The walls in the trailer were thin—didn't even go flush to the ceiling; Beth could see the crack of light that showed over the top. Sometimes she and Geraldine would lie there pretending to be asleep—both of them, Beth knew, listening to the sounds of their parents' lovemaking. They never talked about them; never even admitted they'd heard.

But tonight there were only voices. Soft, tired voices, and although Beth missed a word or two, the conversation was as clear as if her parents were in the room beside her.

"She get all them flowers done, you think?" Her father's voice.

"Looks to me she did." Mother never admitted helping out; it made him angry, Mother working two jobs. " . . . a mind to let her keep the whole payment this time, Ray. She's needing a coat this winter. She could use it."

"Wouldn't hurt her to stay home tomorrow and get herself ahead—have them flowers ready the next time Mrs. Goff wants 'em done."

A sigh. The squeak of the bed as Mother crawled in beside him. More squeaking as she settled into place. Then silence for a time. Beth thought perhaps that was the end of it, when she heard her father continue:

"Day I turned sixteen, my dad told me how much rent I got to pay, and from then on I was a boarder. Earned my keep like everyone else."

"We're not going to charge the kids rent, Ray. Beth turns over half her flower money as it is and don't complain. . . ."

More silence. Then Father's voice again: " . . . was talking to George at the diner yesterday. Told him my oldest girl's turning sixteen in the spring. He says bring her by after her birthday and he'll give her a try as a waitress. Full-time. Minimum wage to start and raises regular if she measures up. . . . Could ride in with me of a morning, work the same shift. Get herself a steady job before all the college kids come back, looking for summer work."

Beth felt as though her lungs had frozen. For a moment a panicky feeling welled up inside her as she struggled for breath. She waited numbly for her mother's reply.

The bed creaked again. Another sigh. "Don't know as she'd put her heart in it," Lorna said at last.

"Don't have to put her heart in it. Put her back to it, like you and me been doing all our lives. Elizabeth thinks she's too good for waitress work, she's another think coming."

Beth's arms fell limply to her sides, her heart pounding. The flashlight rolled down off her lap and settled between her thigh and the mattress, its small circle of light beaming against the quilt over her legs.

She swallowed and swallowed again, not making a sound. But long after the noises in her parents' room had stopped, their voices drifting off into sleep, Beth stared at the wall opposite, at the hole where Geraldine had tried to tack up a photo of Tom Cruise, at the green curtains that were hanging crooked and had never been set right, at the hook where the girls kept their blow dryer . . .

I'm not leaving school when I'm sixteen, she said, making no sound, but forming the words with her lips. She took her pencil and engraved the word *not* on the cover of her notebook, the lead going clear through the cardboard.

You saying no to me, girl? her father would ask if she told him.

And somehow she'd have to get up the courage to say yes.

2

Beth loved the smell of her typing classroom—the ink of typewriter ribbons, the crisp fragrance of new paper, the glue smell of textbooks, and the occasional sweet scent of a girl's perfume—usually Stephanie King's. It was the one place in Crandall High School that Beth felt she belonged.

"Time!" the teacher called, pressing her stopwatch, and all fingers paused in midair. The clackety noise ceased. Beth suspected that the row of students in the back at the new silent models finished a word or two after time was called, but it made no difference. She usually came out ahead of the others for accuracy and number of words typed, though Stephanie was a close second.

"Papers, please," Miss Talbot said, and the papers were pulled from typewriter carriages and passed hand over shoulder to the front of the room.

Beth waited happily, watching the tall, blond teacher, who could have been a New York model if she'd wanted, Beth guessed. Miss Talbot put those papers aside and picked up yesterday's set.

"I was very pleased with your last test, class. You really made my day!" she said, smiling.

Faces smiled back.

"The top speed was Beth Herndon's, at forty-seven words per minute. . . ." She held out Beth's paper, and Beth rose from her seat to go get it. As she walked to the front of the room, she struggled to contain the smile that was rapidly taking over her face. It was no use. When Beth reached the teacher, Miss Talbot said, "You keep this up, you'll be typing eighty words a minute by the end of the semester. Nice work."

Beth flushed and turned back toward her seat, the smile breaking wide open in spite of herself, so that when she passed Stephanie King's desk, she was grinning like a jack-o'-lantern. Stephanie met her eyes and turned away.

She's no cause to be jealous of me, Beth thought as she slipped her paper in her notebook. Stephanie was an honor student and probably going to Morgantown to college when she graduated. She wasn't used to being topped by anyone, Beth knew, least of all a Herndon living out on Shadbush Road. Everything about Stephanie was perfect, from the short blond hair that was cut in layers, like feathers, at the side of her head, to the Reeboks she wore on her feet. Everything about her was perfect, that is, except her typing paper. Helplessly, Beth grinned again out of sheer delight.

Clarice Johns, Beth's closest friend this semester, waited for her at the door after the bell.

"Nothing I like more than walking in through the door

of this class, and nothing I hate worse than leaving," Beth confided.

"Wait till we get to dictaphones," Clarice said. She was taller, a little fuller than Beth, but had the same high cheekbones, as though they'd all been descended from the same grandfather somewhere down the line. "My sister says they can drive you crazier than a loon."

"What's so hard about them?"

"You've got to listen to a tape of somebody reading, and type what he says."

"What if you can't keep up?"

"You can stop it with a foot pedal—turn it on again when you're ready. But Joan's got a boss who talks like his mouth's full of potato; she says you can listen to a word fifty times and still not know what it is. Sometimes she just has to guess." They smiled at the thought. As they approached the gym, Clarice asked, "Going to the Halloween party?"

"What party's that?"

"One the fire department puts on. It's free."

"I don't think so," Beth told her. "Dad's going to be taking us around in the pickup. I've got to paint Betty Jo and Ruth Marie and fix up the others."

"I could ask Joan to come by and get you, if you want to go."

The idea of someone stopping by the trailer had not occurred to Beth—stopping by without an invitation, that is, which she surely never intended to give. Not even to Clarice. The one good thing about not having a telephone was that people didn't call asking if they could come over, and if they tried to look up your address in the phone book, you weren't there.

"I'd better not," Beth said again. "I've got to go along, see that the kids don't fall out of the truck." It sounded like a lame excuse, even to her.

"Lots of nice boys at the firehouse," Clarice prodded.

"I got more boys around me all the time than I can stand, and all of them brothers," Beth told her. Clarice laughed as she went on down the hall, and Beth entered the gym.

It was when she was changing into her shorts and T-shirt in the locker room that Beth realized she felt hot. "Hope to God I'm not getting what Bud had last week," she murmured. She'd already missed a week in September, because of strep throat, and couldn't afford to be sick again.

But she liked gym almost as much as she liked typing, except for the unit on ballroom dancing. Boys and girls were paired off like socks from the dryer, wrapped around each other out there on the gym floor and taught the fox trot, the waltz, and a simple two-step.

"Just in case you ever find yourselves in a situation where they do ballroom dancing," the instructor had said, and everyone hooted. There wasn't a single place in all of Crandall where there was any music but what was on the radio or juke box except for the Marlin Brothers Country Band at a restaurant up near Shady Spring. Five percent of all the boys in Crandall would go into the coal mines, five percent into the lumberyard or gas stations, ten percent would join the service to learn a trade, and all the rest would leave Crandall. Go up to Ohio, maybe. That's what the principal told them once in

21

a school assembly. Maybe they did that kind of dancing in Ohio.

Beth stuffed her clothes into her locker and tied her gym shoes. She herself had never been to Ohio. What came to mind was lowland, a high hill, and bottomland again. Oh-*high*-oh. To-*le*-do, O-*hi*-o. The cities of Ohio were mysterious sounding, very different from Morgantown, Parsons, and Elkins.

Beth had never, in fact, been farther than Hawk's Nest, and that wasn't even a town—just a high place up on a ridge where you went with a sixth-grade science class so you could look out over New River Gorge. So you could learn all the different layers of rock and how they'd been forming for 300 million years. Then back home again over switch-back roads that turned sharply in one direction, then another, and you leaned first toward the window, then the aisle. If there was a logging truck in front of you, any kind of truck, even— grinding and groaning up the hill ahead—you could just kiss the time good-bye. No place to pass. Might as well sit back and enjoy the ride. Past towns with names like Contentment or Chimney Corner, Unincorporated. Past the Lover's Leap Baptist Church. Past Saturday Road and Sunday Road and purple, rock-faced walls of cliffs.

Beth followed the other girls into the gymnasium. Her head had a heavy feel to it, as though she were balancing a cinder block. There was no ballroom dancing today. The boys were back over on their own side of the partition, and rope rings had been lowered from the high ceiling. Beth listened as the instructor described the exercise:

"The object, girls, is to swing rhythmically from one ring to the next. I don't want to see any jerky movements; I don't want to see any awkward kicks. Get your whole body into it, swinging like the pendulum of a clock." The teacher demonstrated, her body moving higher and higher off the floor.

When it was her turn, Beth knew that her movements were jerky, but she loved the feel of her body swaying, her arms stretching, the silent, heavy swing of the rope, the clutch of her fingers on the leather handgrips. When she reached the end of the line, her feet high off the floor, she reversed direction and started back, each ring taking her lower and lower. I'm a hawk, she thought giddily, soaring out above the gorge.

But her head felt hotter still as she tried to review amphibians over lunch. English, biology, and business math yet to go. When she took her biology test, fifth period, she expected a drawing of a frog, with blanks to fill in, labeling its parts. Instead, all the parts of the frog were listed in two long columns, and Beth was supposed to divide them into skeletal system, muscular system, nervous system, and all the other systems that she wasn't at all sure she remembered.

She did the best she could, but when she turned in her paper at the bell, the teacher asked, "Feeling all right, Beth?"

"Head's sort of hot," she told him.

"I thought so." Mr. Emerson reached for his pen and wrote out a pass. "Here. Take this to the nurse. She'll want to check your temperature."

Beth had hoped she could at least hold out until the weekend. Every time she missed school, there was that much more to catch up, and it was hard to study at home. Wordlessly she picked up her books and walked slowly down the corridor toward the health room as the bell rang for the next class and the halls emptied. Miss Talbot and Miss Wentworth, the two most beautiful teachers in the school, were standing outside the office chatting with each other, the bracelets on Miss Wentworth's wrist tinkling delicately as she gestured. Beth felt dowdy by comparison as she passed and ducked into the health room.

The nurse was young, small, and freckled, and looked to be scarcely older than Beth herself, though Beth knew she was twenty-four and married. She didn't dress in a white uniform, either, like Mrs. Bogden back in junior high; she greeted Beth in gray slacks and a pink sweater.

"Here's a fever if I ever saw one," she said, putting a hand on Beth's forehead. She took a thermometer from a jar of antiseptic. "You're . . .?"

"Beth Herndon," Beth said, sitting down and letting the thermometer in under her tongue.

"Oh, yes. You had strep last month, didn't you?" The nurse opened the file drawer, found Beth's card, and studied it a moment. Finally, checking her watch, she took out the thermometer. "A hundred and two. Anything hurt? Ears? Throat?"

"Just my head," Beth told her. "I know it's the flu. Bud had it last week, and Lyle and Geraldine the week before."

"Brothers and sisters?"

Beth nodded again.

"Well, there's a lot of it going around, but I'm going to take another throat culture, just to make sure it's not our old

24

friend again. I know how you love this," the nurse said, taking a long cotton swab from a jar.

When Beth opened her mouth, she felt like gagging already, and did so when the nurse swabbed the back of her throat. But Mrs. Lester was fast.

"Done," she said, transferring the smear to a glass slide and putting Beth's name on it.

Beth wished now that she hadn't mentioned the flu, afraid the nurse might insist she stay home a week, as she had before. "I'll probably feel lots better by tomorrow," she said hopefully. "Mom says every kind of sickness there is, we invite it in and pass it around between the ten of us. But we don't any of us hang on to it very long."

"Ten children in your family?"

"No, only eight."

"All from the same parents?"

The question stopped Beth a moment. "Yes, ma'am," she said in answer.

"What are their ages, Beth?" The nurse sat down at her desk now like she had all the time in the world. Her eyes seemed kind, and that's why Beth trusted her, she thought later.

"I'm the oldest," she said. "Douglas is the baby. He was just three. The rest are every age there is, almost, in between."

"Well, let me check your neck now—see what your lymph nodes are up to." The nurse swiveled her chair around, and her fingers were smooth and cool on the sides of Beth's neck; they smelled of antiseptic. "I can feel some enlargement. Anybody at home to come get you?"

25

"Dad doesn't get home till three-thirty, and he's got the truck."

"Well, the bus will get you there sooner than that, but I hate to put you on it, because you'll spread those germs around."

"I'll keep my mouth shut," Beth promised, and they both laughed.

Mrs. Lester made a note on Beth's card, and then, so smoothly that one word seemed to flow into the next, without even looking up, she said, "Eight children is a lot for one woman to bear, Beth. Your mother must be awfully tired."

"We all help out," Beth said, still trusting.

"I suppose she's talked to a clinic? There *is* something she could do to keep from getting pregnant again."

The words, to Beth, seemed to lie in a jumble around her, unassembled, out of place. And before she could line them up, put them together, before she could answer or even think, the nurse had changed the subject: "You lie down on the cot here until school's over. Just slip off your shoes and pull the blanket over you if you're cold. I'll draw the curtain in case we get visitors."

Beth mechanically took off her shoes.

"Do you have a thermometer at home?"

"We borrow Mrs. Maxwell's when we need it," Beth said.

"Well, don't come back to school—don't even *think* about coming back—until your temperature's down to at least ninety-nine. And if you feel any worse tomorrow, you ought to call the doctor. Okay?"

Beth nodded.

"You have a family doctor?"

Beth nodded again and lay down, reaching for the blanket as if for protection, but not from cold. When they absolutely had to, they called Mrs. Maxwell's doctor on Mrs. Maxwell's phone. Beth wasn't about to tell the nurse that.

Mrs. Lester pulled the faded green curtain around the cot, and Beth found herself enveloped in shadow.

"And drink all the water and juice you can hold," Mrs. Lester was saying from her desk. "Help flush those germs out of your system."

There were sounds of file drawers opening and closing, papers being shuffled, humming, a phone call, a student coming in with a nosebleed, another needing a note. . . .

Just after the biology test, Beth had felt tired enough to sleep. If she had lain down right then, she might have drifted off, but now she stared up at the ceiling, unblinking, and tried to recount the conversation word for word. Mrs. Bogden at the junior high would never have said that. Would never even have asked those kinds of questions. The crack in Beth's world was growing wider still, and it wasn't just the kids on the school bus who were looking in, but everyone, it seemed.

Over the weekend, Ruth Marie and Mother became ill also, and it was Tuesday before Beth's temperature was down to 99 degrees—99½ degrees, actually. Beth stopped at the water fountain in the hallway and sloshed cold water around her mouth and under her tongue before she went into the health room to have her temperature rechecked. This time she volunteered no information at all about her family—who else

27

was sick and who was not—and answered the nurse's questions with a simple "Yes, ma'am," or "No, ma'am," and was allowed to return to class. But first she stopped at the front desk, where Clarice helped out in the mornings.

"Boy, did you ever pick a time to be sick!" Clarice said, checking Beth in on the attendance sheet. "You should have seen that test we had in English! We've got another one next week on clauses, and then we have to write a paper on our career goals, using one of every kind of clause there is."

"I don't want to hear about it," Beth groaned. "See you in typing class," she said, and fled. There were tests and assignments to be made up in each of her classes, a pop quiz in history. She had received a *D* on her biology test, but when report cards came out the day before Halloween, she'd gotten a *C-* in the class. A *C* in English, a *B* in business math, a *B* in phys ed, a *C* in history, and there, for the first time Beth could remember, an *A+* on her report card. In typing.

She laid the report card on the dinette table when she got home, where her mother would be sure to see it. When the others came in, they added their report cards to hers, and as Mrs. Herndon stirred the chili that night, she picked them up one by one and looked them over.

"Lyle, what's this *F* in earth science?" she called out above the noise of the TV. "You fixing to do the same in junior high you did back in sixth grade, barely get yourself promoted?"

"It's *hard*, Ma! He don't like me, anyways. Calls on me near every day, twice sometimes, and don't hardly call on some of the other kids at all."

"Wants to see if you got any more sense in your head than you did the day before, that's why," Mother said. She put Lyle's report card down and picked up another. "Now Ruth Marie got herself three *B*s."

Beth sat in front of the TV waiting, Douglas on her lap. Any minute her mother would see her card, any minute now she'd announce the *A*+. Mrs. Herndon was looking at it, Beth could tell. She was holding the very last card in the bunch. She stared at it a good long while without comment, then glanced at Beth and gave her a little smile. "Well!" she said, and put it aside.

At mealtime, Beth seated the three youngest on the sofa with bowls of chili in their laps and a box of crackers between them, then took her place at the card table with her father, Geraldine, and Lyle. Mother sat at the dinette with the others. The report cards had been moved to the top of the refrigerator, where they fluttered and shifted each time the door was opened.

"I got three *B*s on my report card, Dad," Ruth Marie announced smugly.

"Good," said her father. "You keep it up now, hear?"

"Ruth Marie and Beth and Bud did all right," said Mrs. Herndon. "It's Lyle and Geraldine and Betty Jo in need of study."

Did all right? That's all Mother had to say? Beth swallowed, waiting. But Mother had reached across the dinette table to smack Betty Jo's hands for wiping them on her T-shirt.

Suddenly Beth got up from her chair and went to the refrigerator. She sorted through the report cards until she found

29

her own. Then she took some tape from the drawer, stuck the card to her shirt front, and sat back down at the table. Geraldine giggled.

"What the heck's that?" Beth's father asked.

Now Ruth Marie was giggling, too, from the other table. Beth herself suppressed a smile.

"My report card," she said in answer.

"You got somethin' you want the world to see?"

"Beth got an $A+$ in typing," Ruth Marie warbled, and Beth knew she'd already peeked.

Beth grinned and glanced shyly around at the others who were looking at her, but Mother continued eating.

"What'd you get in your other classes?" asked Father.

Stung, Beth pulled the report card off her shirt and thrust it at him.

Ray Herndon squinted. "Print's too small to read," he said.

Geraldine took it from him and read the grades aloud.

Beth's father took a long, slow drink of milk. "Seems to me you don't get any better grades those other classes, you'd be better off quittin' school," he said. "Can pick up a typing course anywhere; don't have to go to school three more years to learn it."

Beth felt hot prickles of anger on the sides of her head. "You've got to have a high-school diploma for the *good* typing jobs," she told him.

"What makes you think there's any that pays near enough to make a living?"

"There's some! Miss Talbot puts want ads on the bulletin board to show us. Right now they're looking for a typist at the real estate company. You've just got to be ready when the right job comes along. I'll have as good a chance as anyone else if I get my diploma. *Better*, maybe."

"Listen, Beth," her father said, and this time his voice was gentle. "You can earn the same in tips alone in some of those fancy restaurant places. Don't have to have no diploma, either. You could start out at the diner, get yourself some experience, and move on up to the Ridgeview Restaurant over on Route Twenty." He studied her earnestly.

"I want to finish high school, Dad," she said.

"Well," Ray said slowly, "what you want and what you do is sometimes two different things entirely." He pushed his plate away and sat staring out the window, arms resting on the table.

Lyle got in the act. "Sure would be easier to do reports if we had some encyclopedias around here. That's how come I got a *F* in earth science, Dad. Didn't have anything to use."

This time Beth's father turned his head swiftly. "You got a school library, don't you?"

"Yeah, but it's hard to use the library during the day, or sometimes the book you want is taken. And if we stay after school to use it, we miss the bus, and then we have to call Maxwells' and ask you to come for us."

"Never said I wouldn't, did I? You think every boy going to school has his own set of encyclopedias?"

"No, it would just make things easier, is all I'm saying," said Lyle.

"And who the hell told you life was easy?" Ray Herndon was glaring now. "You ever hear that from my lips? You

31

think your mother and I got it easy? You kids don't know what work is, I swear to God you don't. Want a set of encyclopedias at home so's you don't have to use the library; want a typing job so's you can sit down all day, don't have to carry trays to the kitchen."

"I never *said* that!" Beth flared, her eyes shooting sparks of their own. "I want to do typing 'cause I'm *good* at it! Because I could move up, *make* something of myself."

What frightened her next was not her father's reply, but the lack of it. Their eyes met, and yet he said nothing. But Beth had never seen his eyes look so dark. With hurt? With anger? She couldn't tell

The TV blared away on the side of the room where the three on the sofa sat watching, but it sounded unnatural without the usual accompaniment of family chatter.

It was Mother who started the conversation again. "You tell me where the money's going to come from for a set of encyclopedias, I'll buy them," she said. "What do you want to give up, Lyle? New clothes? Wear the ones you got all through junior high and high school? You show me where we can cut, I'll do it. Your father works as hard as any man on Earth. You kids want a set of encyclopedias, *you* buy them."

The rest of the meal was eaten in silence, except for the clink of spoons in bowls, a belch from Shirley on the couch, the crunch of crackers, and the ever-present noise of the TV. One by one, people finished, put their dishes in the sink, and drifted off, except for Bud and Ruth Marie, whose job it was to do the dishes that week.

Beth put on her jacket and went across the road to walk off the tension, kicking at the clumps of leaves from the basswoods and tulip poplars, trampling them underfoot as she tried to sort things through. She was surpised at her mother's outburst, at the way the argument over her report card had escalated. She hadn't meant to start any criticism of their father. None of them really expected him to bring home the *World Book Encyclopedia*. Lyle was just making a point, that's all.

Her father *did* work hard. She knew it. Being the oldest, Beth was the only child in the family who remembered when they had lived in a standard-size trailer behind the Texaco station in Crandall. About the time Ruth Marie was born, however, Father had hurt his back in the lumberyard and could no longer do heavy lifting. With his disability insurance, he had bought a second trailer to attach to the first, moved them both across the river, and gotten a job as grill man in the diner. He didn't smoke, didn't drink, didn't gamble, and the only amusement he allowed himself once a week was a few games of duckpin bowling—the most his back could take—with some friends. Not one of the Herndons would have deprived their dad of that.

How many other children had encyclopedias at home? her father had asked. Not that many, Beth agreed. You couldn't call the Herndons poor as long as they had jobs and a roof over their heads, could you? Poor people lived on the streets; she'd seen those people on the news, pushing their possessions around in shopping carts and sleeping on heating grates— people who lined up at missions for a meal. Her father shouldn't get upset just because he couldn't afford encyclopedias.

There were footsteps from behind, the sound of running feet through the leaves, and then Geraldine caught up with her, breathless.

"Wonder what got into *them*!" she exclaimed. Geraldine's sandy hair was almost as long and as straight as Beth's, and her eyebrows came delicately together over the bridge of her nose.

"I don't know." Beth shook her head. "Just can't figure what Dad wants from me. Only *A+* in the whole family, ever, and he won't even look at it. And Ma didn't turn any handsprings, either. Almost like I've done something I've got to hang my head over."

"Well, if it was *my* report card he'd taken out after, there would have been a whole lot more shouting," Geraldine said, as if to comfort her. "Two *D*s and all the rest *C*s. If Dad wants *me* to leave school when I'm sixteen, he sure won't get no argument."

"Gerry, I want to graduate and he doesn't want me to. Simple as that," Beth said. "How many other fathers you suppose there are who want their oldest daughter to leave school? He never talked like that before. Seems like the last couple years he's just grown cold to me."

"Lyle pushed his button, is all." Geraldine thrust her hands in the pockets of her jacket and hunched her shoulders against the chill. "That truck's causing him fits. Every time he turns around, something else is wrong with it. You ask Dad for anything these days, he'll take a bite out of you."

"I expect that's it."

They walked side by side for a while along the river, the sky growing darker, lights flickering here and there on the high hill behind Crandall on the opposite bank. Every so often a strong breeze blew up, bringing with it the smell of wood smoke.

Beth's sympathies turned from herself to her sister, and she felt a pang at Geraldine's willingness to drop out of school so readily. In some ways they were alike, but in others they were very different. Beth couldn't believe that she herself was much smarter than Geraldine. Some, maybe. It probably had more to do with being the first baby born into a family. That child was bound to get more attention, more time—so maybe she'd grown up feeling better about herself, more determined to *be* somebody.

But if that was true, if her parents had loved her so and encouraged her when she was little, why did they seem to be holding back now? How was it she could remember compliments from her dad when she was five, six, and seven, making her feel special, somehow, but almost none lately? Maybe her grades *weren't* as good as they used to be, but each child born into the family took another chunk out of Beth's time and energy. Couldn't her father understand that?

"Beth," Geraldine said suddenly, "I been kissed."

Beth glanced over. "You bragging or complaining?"

Geraldine laughed giddily. "Just telling you, is all."

"Who by?" Beth laughed, too.

"Jack Carey. Boy from school."

"When do you ever see a boy he's got a chance to kiss you?"

"We eat lunch together and walk around outside after. Oh, Beth, he's the cutest!"

They walked on a little farther in a crunchy duet of dried leaves underfoot, while Geraldine described Jack Carey from the color of his hair to the size of his feet.

"Sounds to me like he ought to be in the movies," Beth said finally.

"I'll get a picture of him. You'll see."

"Mom know?"

"She'd kill me. Jack's going to be at the fire department party tomorrow night, though, so I won't be going out trick-or-treating. Why don't you come, too, Beth? See him your-self?"

"Who'll look after the others?"

"Lyle can do it. Ruth Marie's like a little old lady, anyway. Let her play mother for the night."

"Well, maybe," Beth said. They went as far as the falls, which wasn't much of a falls at all when the river was low, then turned back. On the other side of Shadbush Road, every house was ready and waiting for Halloween. Stuffed dummies in overalls hung from trees, sat on porches, even perched on bicycles out in the yards. Jack-o'-lanterns waited on steps for the visitors who would come the following night.

"Just don't go too fast," Beth warned.

Geraldine slowed her steps, then understood what was meant. "Can't do much more than kiss at school," she said.

"Thirteen years old, that's enough," said Beth.

"Fourteen in December," Gerry reminded her.

"It's still enough," said Beth, and they laughed.

When they got back to the trailer, Betty Jo and Bud were pasting cats, cut out of newsprint and colored black, on all the windows. Last year's decorations had been put into place three weeks ago, but still the children thought of more. You couldn't do enough for Halloween.

Beth followed Geraldine into the main room, where Shirley and Douglas were trying to shove each other off the couch.

"I won't be going out trick-or-treating this year, Dad," Gerry said. "I'm going to the fire department party with some friends from school. One of the fathers is going to drive us over, and I asked Beth to go with us."

Ray Herndon looked up from the lamp socket he was repairing in his lap. "Funny nobody mentioned it to me when we talked about it the other night. I thought you were all eager to go out again in the truck."

"*We* are!" cried Bud and Betty Jo and Ruth Marie together.

"Well, it's me that won't be going this time, 'cause I feel like I'm comin' down with whatever the rest of you had," Father said. "Had a jackhammer going in my head all day, so I asked Harless Prather to take you out in his truck. He's coming by tomorrow about seven."

"Who's Harless Prather?" Geraldine asked, going to the refrigerator and taking out the rest of her chili she'd saved from dinner.

"Fella who delivers bread and rolls to the diner. I told him Beth would go along, show him the houses to stop at."

"Lyle can show him," Beth protested, suddenly wanting

37

very much to go to the party. Clarice and her sister would be there, and if even *Geraldine* was going . . .

"Lyle's going to have his hands full just getting the others to the front door and back," said Mother. "Shirley and Douglas want to go this year, and there's one person's energy right there, just looking out for them."

"But Ruth Marie. . . ," Beth began.

Her father turned on her suddenly. "I said you was going, Beth, because I didn't know no different. You got plans from now on, you let me in on 'em."

Beth looked pleadingly at her mother. It wasn't even so much that she wanted to go to the party; she just wanted a choice. But Mother was intent on the ironing she was doing for Mrs. Goff, and from the look of the heap in the basket, she'd be at it both this night and the next. There was no way Mother could go.

Beth moved numbly toward the couch, picked up Douglas, who was standing now with his head on a cushion, thumb in his mouth, and carted him off toward a back bedroom on the other side, which he shared with Bud. Ruth Marie, Betty Jo, and Shirley shared the fourth bedroom.

Silently Beth removed her little brother's pants, put a diaper on him for overnight, and tucked him into his cot by the window. She sat for a while rubbing his back as he settled in, as she did every night, but her mind was on her father. At what point had he begun to dislike her so? He was only forty, eight years older than Lorna, but to Beth he looked fifty at least. Sixty, even. His face was deeply lined, like the rings on a tree stump, one line for every hard year of his life. Whenever Beth conjured him up, he had a face that looked like worry.

But there *had* been times he'd held her, sung to her. Used to tell her bear stories—scared her so badly she could hardly sleep—and the following night she'd be waiting for the next installment. Took her fishing when she was ten. Taught her to bait her own hook.

When was it, exactly, that he'd started finding fault—holding back praise, no matter what she did? Worse yet, Mother usually agreed with him, if only by her silence.

In the darkness of the bedroom, Beth could make out the shapes of boxes stacked in one corner. Half the room, in fact, had been turned into an open closet for the whole family, with clothes piled everywhere. The cots for Bud and Douglas seemed almost an afterthought, shoved against one wall. Beth's hand caressed her small brother's shoulders, and she ran one finger along his neck. If each succeeding child in the family got less time and attention than the one before, then Douglas would be shortchanged the most.

Through the open window, Beth heard the horn of Amtrak's *Cardinal*, which came through Crandall. At one end of the line was Chicago; at the other, New York City. Someday she'd be on that train, going where, she didn't know.

3

It did not rain on Halloween. The sky was overcast, dark as syrup, blotting out even a hint of moon. But it was warm enough that the children could get by with only sweaters beneath their costumes, and after going next door to trick-or-treat the Maxwells, they whirled and pranced as they waited for Harless Prather and his truck.

"Mrs. Maxwell said to watch out for witches," Shirley said soberly, stopping a moment to rest. "There aren't any witches, are there, Mama?"

"None I ever saw," Lorna answered.

"You might not know if you *did* see one," said Ruth Marie. "There's only one way to tell if somebody's a witch. Mrs. Maxwell told it to me."

"How?" asked Bud and Betty Jo together.

"You've got to sit her down and then you slip a fork under the chair and if she's a real witch she can't get up."

Shirley and Bud exchanged wary glances.

Beth gave a wry smile. "Come here, Betty Jo, let me fix that scarf." She adjusted the gypsy bandanna with the loop earrings sewn at the sides. "You don't keep it straight, it'll look like your ears are lopsided."

She also pinned the black-stocking cat's tail back on Shirley; it came off every time the little girl climbed up on the sofa with Douglas to look out the window.

Beth had dressed the younger children, but she spoke only to them, avoiding her parents. Ruth Marie could have been assigned to watch out for Douglas, Betty Jo for Shirley. There was no reason for keeping Beth home from the party except to make her miserable. Mother, she could tell, was having second thoughts about it, the way she kept throwing compliments Beth's way.

"Now just look at that face!" Mother had exclaimed after Beth had made up Douglas to look like a clown. "Nobody in the family do as good as you do, Beth, at painting faces." She had set down the iron and admired each costumed child. But Beth turned her back and sat watching TV. Silence had become a weapon in the house.

The other person keeping quiet was Geraldine, who had taken refuge in the bedroom right after supper as though afraid that any minute her parents would see the injustice of allowing her to go while Beth could not. Beth did not hold it against her, however. Trying to read their parents' minds these days was like trying to make sense of the weather; turn on you faster than you could blink.

Lyle and Bud were out by the road in their tramp costumes, acting like they were hitching rides, then laughing and backing off if a car stopped.

Ruth Marie sat daintily by the door in an old rayon robe that Beth had transformed into a Japanese kimono. "Harless Prather's going to go right on by, the way Lyle and Bud's scaring off cars," she protested.

Lorna Herndon put down the iron and went to the door. "You! Lyle Thomas! Bud Charles! Get yourselves in here!"

The boys loped inside, big patches sewn on their jeans, faces smeared with coal.

"He don't get here soon, folks'll start turning off their porch lights," Bud complained, looking at the clock, which now read seven-twenty.

Beth fought against the wish that the man *wouldn't* come —that Dad would have to take them out after all. Then she saw headlights slowing down and turning in.

"He's here!" Betty Jo screeched, but it was a car.

A horn sounded, and Geraldine flew out of the bedroom as though shot from a gun.

"Good Lord in heaven!" Ray said, staring at her as she grabbed her coat. "What we got here?"

Beth stared, too, and couldn't help smiling. Geraldine had used green food dye to color half her hair, and lard to make it stand up in spikes around her head. She was wearing her black jeans and pullover, with earrings of safety pins.

"She's a punk!" Bud sang out. "Wow!"

"Somethin' not even a cat would bother to drag in," Father said, trying to coax a smile, it seemed, from Beth.

But as Geraldine sailed out the door, Beth's bitterness surfaced again. She'd already spent ten years of her life raising babies not even her own, and it looked as though her parents had her figured for another ten. They figured wrong.

More headlights on the road, slowing down, waiting until the car with Geraldine in it had left. Then a pickup pulled in the small clearing in front of the trailers.

"That's Prather's truck," Father said, going over to the window. "You all behave yourselves, hear?" He took two aspirin from the bottle in his hand and gulped them down.

A truck door slammed, then there was the sound of heavy-booted footsteps on the ground, a rap on the screen.

"Got any ghosts and goblins in here?" came a voice, and a moment later a tall, thin, young man stepped into the room. Beth stared. In place of some potbellied, middle-aged man, this one was wearing hunting boots and jeans, a red-and-black-plaid jacket, and had straight, short hair the color of orange peel. His eyes traveled about the room, taking in each child's costume in turn and passed over Beth as though she weren't even there. Then suddenly his eyes were on her again. *Whoa,* they seemed to say. *Who's this?*

Beth felt her face flush. She got up quickly and reached for the old jacket she'd thrown on the sofa.

Ray, in his stocking feet, padded over to Harless.

"Well, these here are my kids—most of 'em, anyways. Lorna, this is Harless Prather, bread man for the diner."

"You sure took on a chore," Mother said, smiling.

"Nothin' better to do on Halloween." Harless grinned, and Beth noticed that his teeth were good. "Figured maybe your kids would share their Hershey's bars with me."

"*I* will!" said Betty Jo.

Harless smiled. "Who I got riding up front?"

"Beth can take the two young ones on her lap, and the others can ride in back," Dad said. He turned to Lyle and

Ruth Marie. "You two watch out for Bud and Betty Jo now. Don't go horsin' around, fall out and crack your head. They give you any trouble, Harless, you bring 'em right back."

"I'll crack me a few heads together myself," Harless said. He gave Beth a full smile this time. "Ready to go?"

In answer, Beth leaned over Douglas, grabbing his arm. "You got to go to the bathroom? You need to go, you tell me now. Don't you wait till we get in the truck."

He shook his head, struggling to break free.

"I put a diaper on him just in case," Mother said.

Harless held the door open. "Nice out tonight," he said, and his eyes followed Beth as she slipped past him. She could feel them on her still as she went to the truck.

She helped Shirley climb up first, then got in herself, Douglas in her arms. Outside, Harless Prather was helping the other four into the open back. Then he came around to the driver's side and slid onto the seat.

"So how you all doing?" he asked, sticking his key in the ignition.

Beth nudged Shirley, who was squeezed in between them. "What do you say when somebody asks you a question, Shirl?"

"Fiiiine!" the little girl said, her feet wiggling.

Harless smiled and started the engine. When traffic was clear, he backed slowly out onto the road.

"You some kind of ventriloquist?" he asked, glancing over at Beth. "Seem like every time I say somethin' to you, you get one of the babies to answer."

Beth felt her cheeks flame, but she smiled a little. "Didn't know who you were talking to."

"Well, I got a choice between a little girl not even in school yet and a young woman, I'll take the woman."

"She's fifteen," offered Shirley.

"Fifteen and a half," Beth corrected, then blushed fiercely. As if he cared.

"Where you want to go now?" Harless asked as the truck moved down the road. "You want to stop, you sing out."

In the back of the truck, Lyle and Bud were braying like dogs.

"Kept my hounds home, figured they'd scare the babies. Now seems like I picked up a couple more," Harless said.

"Lyle and Bud are always acting crazy," Beth told him.

"I've got brothers, so I know," he answered.

Beth pointed. "Right up ahead, house with the side porch. You can stop there if you want. We'll walk on to the other houses and then come back to the truck."

Harless pulled off onto the shoulder. "I'll be here playing my radio."

Taking Douglas and Shirley with her, Beth walked across the road. The others had already climbed out and were waiting for them, Lyle and Bud down on all fours now, noses pointed toward the sky, howling like wolves.

"Sound like near idiots," Beth said.

"I *told* them to stop!" said Ruth Marie.

"Well, Harless thinks you're crazy," Beth added.

"Oh, he does not!" said Lyle. "It's Halloween! Listen, Beth, doesn't this sound real?" And he gave a mournful, wavering howl that got a dog going in someone's backyard. Beth had to laugh.

They tramped up the small rise to the first house, and Bud banged on the door.

"Trick-or-treat!" they all shouted as the door opened and a woman appeared with a bowl of candy.

They walked on to the next house and the next, and when someone gave Beth a Mars bar, she plunked it in Harless's hand when she got back in the truck.

"It's not a Hershey's, but it's close," she said.

"It'll do," he told her. "Want half?"

She shook her head. "Drive on down to the trailer court. After that you can go back the other way to Goffs' Motel. We usually end up there." She unwrapped one of Douglas's candies for him and another for Shirley.

On the way to the trailer court, she asked, "This the truck you deliver bread in?"

"Nope." Harless grinned. "I drive the company truck on my rounds. This Chevy's my own set of wheels."

"Then how come Dad knew you had a pickup?"

"'Cause it's all I ever talk about when I come in the diner. Be payin' for it till I'm a old man." Harless laughed. "Guess you figure I'm a old man already."

"Not really," Beth said, smiling a little.

"How old you think I am?"

She shrugged. "How should I know?"

"You can make a guess, can't you?"

"Thirty-seven," Shirley said, and Beth and Harless laughed.

"Twenty-three," Beth guessed.

"Close. Be twenty-three my next birthday."

They rode on a way in silence. Harless turned up his radio finally and tapped his finger to the music.

At the trailer court the Herndons separated, Lyle going off to the homes of friends, Ruth Marie, Bud, and Betty Jo going to others. Beth found she was stuck again with Douglas and Shirley. The cat's tail had come off Shirley and she'd lost her broom-straw whiskers on one side.

"You got to itch, you tell me where," Beth said. "You go scratching yourself, you'll lose all the paint I put on you." She looked back over her shoulder at Harless as they started off. "Sure you haven't got anything better to do than ride us around? Seems a waste."

He leaned his arm on the window of the truck. "I wouldn't say that," he told her.

He sure did a lot of smiling, Beth thought; grinning, more like it. They were both grinners, she and him. She waited while Shirley went up the steps of a trailer, Douglas following behind, one step at a time, in shoes that were much too large for him. Bet Harless was just thrilled out of his mind when Dad asked him to take us out, she mused as the obligatory candy was passed around.

They went to only three other homes in the trailer court; then Douglas said he was cold, so they walked back to the truck. Harless had the music turned down real low this time—slow music—a woman moaning about love.

From the way Douglas sat in her lap, his head heavy in the crook of her arm, Beth could tell that he was tuckered out.

47

Shirley had grown quiet, also, and sat sucking noisily on a caramel, swallowing with loud, satisfied sighs.

"Sure don't take much to make you happy, does it?" Harless asked her, and then, to Beth, "Your dad has himself a whole lot of children, don't he?" He stretched one arm along the back of the seat.

Beth nodded. "How many in your family?"

"Five altogether. Three kids, all of 'em boys. Mom says she knew if she tried for a girl she'd end up with four boys, and that was about three more than she could stand."

"You know my dad long?"

"Been delivering to the diner about a year. Nice man. Works hard. Probably worth a lot more than they pay him."

"True about everyone around here, isn't it?"

"Yeah. I reckon so."

The silence had begun to get awkward. From somewhere up in the trees, a barred owl gave its mournful hoot. Douglas was fast asleep now, his body heavy and unmoving in Beth's lap, and the way Shirley leaned against her arm, it felt as if she were sleepy, too, leaving Beth to carry on a conversation with a man she scarcely knew. If Harless was twenty-two, that made him seven years older than she was. Why, if he was a college man, he'd be graduated. Probably had a girlfriend somewhere waiting for him to get this little job done with and over to her house.

Just when Beth was about to suggest that they forget going on to Goffs', she could hear Lyle braying again, laughter, running feet, and then thuds and scrapes as the four climbed into the back of the truck.

"Ready!" Bud yelled, so Harless turned the truck around,

passed the trailer court again, passed the single houses, passed the Herndons' and the Maxwells' trailers, heading toward the bridge into town.

Goffs' Motel and Restaurant was just over the bridge—a brown-shingled, low-frame building with a metal sign out by the road. The rooms behind it used to be separate cabins for the tourists who came to see the falls, but now the cabins had been joined by a common front, and the rail fence around the property gave it the unlikely appearance of a ranch right there at the intersection.

There was a large paper pumpkin pasted on the motel office door, and a hand-lettered sign that said WE WANT TO BE-WITCH YOU ON HALLOWEEN. The Herndons trooped in. Mrs. Goff was a short, buxom woman, with gray hair swooped up at the sides and long, jangling earrings hanging from her earlobes.

"My gracious alive!" she exclaimed, putting her hands to her face, and tried to guess each child. Douglas, in Beth's arms, lifted his head long enough to accept a piece of candy, then snuggled down again on Beth's shoulder.

"Harless Prather, what in the world are you doing out with this bunch?" Mrs. Goff asked, noticing him back in the doorway. "You want some licorice, too?"

Beth turned, surprised he had followed them in. More surprised still to see his face turn bright red.

"Keep me out of mischief," Harless said awkwardly.

"Now *that* will take some doing!" Mrs. Goff teased. "You tell your boss about those burned rolls he sent me?"

"They'll take it off your bill," Harless said. "I already talked to the manager."

"Then that'll set it right," Mrs. Goff told him.

Lyle and Bud were already fooling around with the snack machine near the door, checking to see if there was any change in the coin return, and Beth was eager to get them outside again. Then Harless said, "You real busy in the restaurant tonight, or you think we could have a table?"

Lyle and Bud turned around and stared at Harless. All the Herndons were staring.

"We already had our supper," Ruth Marie said politely.

"So did I, but that was two hours ago. I'm emptier'n a rain barrel in August." Harless turned to Mrs. Goff again. "Think we'd scare off your customers if we went in?"

"Oh, posh, it's Halloween!" the woman said. "You just come along." She picked up a bunch of menus at the door of the dining room and motioned them to follow.

Betty Jo and Ruth Marie looked at Beth uncertainly. They had never eaten in Goffs' Restaurant in their lives. The only place they had *ever* eaten out as a family, in fact, was Burger King. Never in a restaurant with paper menus. But Harless was already herding Lyle and Bud through the doorway, so there was nothing to do but go in.

"Harless," Beth whispered when they reached a long table over by the window, "I didn't bring any money."

"No need," he said, pulling out a chair for her. "Got paid yesterday."

Beth looked helplessly around the table where the others were sliding shyly into chairs, eyes wide with delight. "Yes, but there's seven of us!" she protested.

"And I can eat more than the seven of you together."

"Daddy know you're doing this?"

"What your daddy don't know he can't say a word against now, can he?" Harless answered.

Mrs. Goff was wheeling a high chair over for Douglas, who was staring dazedly around. There were only two other tables of customers, and they smiled at the Herndons, laughing at the coal dust on the boys' faces.

"You all order anything you want," Harless said as Mrs. Goff distributed the menus.

But Beth looked fiercely around the table. "We are *not* ordering supper," she said softly. "Get yourselves some dessert or something."

The older ones opened their menus quietly, eyes traveling down the list of choices.

"You know what I'm hungry for?" Harless was saying, running a hand through his orange-red hair, which lay down under his fingers, then sprang right up again. "A quarter fried chicken and some fries. Now if I can eat all that, Lyle here can eat a hamburger or something."

"*Can* I, Beth?" Lyle asked, leaning over and looking at her down the table.

"If you're sure you want it," she murmured.

When the waitress came over with her pad, Beth said, "Just a dish of chocolate ice cream, please. Shirley and Douglas here will have strawberry."

"And fries!" Shirley added. The waitress smiled and wrote it down.

Lyle ordered the steak-and-cheese sandwich, avoiding Beth's eyes, and then the others placed their orders: "A grilled cheese sandwich and a 7-Up," "Chocolate cake . . ."

"I want biscuits and gravy," Bud sang out when the waitress got to him. Beth closed her eyes.

"Well, I'll just see what we can do about that," the waitress said. The couple in the next booth laughed aloud, and Beth felt her cheeks burning.

"You okay?" Harless asked her.

"Just a little hot."

"I could maybe open a window."

"No, I'm fine, really."

As if to make up for their indiscretions on the menu, the Herndon children ate politely, softly, eyes looking from their plates to their napkins to Beth and back again.

"Bet this sure made a hole in your paycheck," Beth said when the bill came.

"Hey, I enjoyed it!" Harless told her. "Didn't you?"

"Yes, I did," Beth said. "Thanks."

She took Shirley and Douglas to the rest room, and when they went outside again, Harless was standing by his truck while the others chased each other around the parking lot.

"We just took a vote," Harless told her, "and seems like we're goin' to ride into Crandall, do the business district."

"Harless, you don't have to do that!" Beth said urgently. Only once that she could remember had they ever persuaded their father to take them into town on Halloween. The merchants were a good-humored lot and kept a stock of candy on hand, but the logistics of herding the children around Crandall, from store to store, was something else.

"Get food in my stomach, I'm good for another couple hours," Harless said.

So Beth got into the truck again with Shirley and Douglas, and they moved out toward the road.

Even here, where there weren't sidewalks yet, small groups of parents and costumed children made their way into town —the parents with flashlights or sticks to ward off stray dogs, the children holding empty grocery sacks or pillow cases. Other pickups joined the procession of traffic into Crandall, each with its load of children in the back, and the youngsters hooted and yelped at each other.

Beth began to feel glad that they had come and smiled at Harless the next time he looked over. Douglas was asleep again, so she put him on the seat between them, his head resting heavily against her, and let Shirley sit on her lap instead. She pointed out the Halloween decorations in the window of the Super Dollar and laughed with Harless at the two boys going down the sidewalk like Siamese twins, with a box around them for a body. Shirley screeched with delight, but Douglas slept on, his legs, limp as old socks, dangling over the edge of the seat.

Harless pulled his truck into a space in front of the savings and loan, then hopped out.

"Look here," he said to the others, and Beth saw him point toward the clock on the building. "It's five of nine, and I figure you can make most of the stores and be back here by nine-thirty. That okay? Give you time?"

They agreed, but Beth rolled down her window even farther. "Lyle," she yelled. "Ruth Marie. You come here."

The children came.

"Lyle, you and Ruth Marie got to keep the others with

53

you and take Shirley. I'll stay here with Douglas, but I want the five of you to keep together. You hear, now? Don't you leave Shirley behind."

She opened the door so that Shirley could climb out, then turned partway around herself and let her legs hang out the open door. "Don't you get lost, either," she yelled after Lyle, who only gave her a look of disgust and started off toward the movie theater where the woman in the ticket window was giving out peanut-butter kisses.

The night was warm enough to leave the truck door open, so Beth rested one arm on the back of the seat and watched the parade of children on the sidewalk. Harless came around and leaned against the truck next to her, so close that Beth could have reached out and touched his hair with her fingers.

Only at Christmas had Beth ever seen so many people on the sidewalks in Crandall. Perhaps it was the warm night that brought them out, but there were old people, too, sitting on the bench in front of the one-room library and along the low wall by the police station, laughing and pointing out the children, enjoying the show.

The 8:26 westbound was just coming in. Beth could see the bright beam of its light as it came around the bend on the tracks below, rolling up to the old red-brick station. It would be trying to make up time from here on—sailing through a tip of Kentucky, on into Ohio, then Indiana and Illinois.

"You think they do any different in Ohio?" Beth mused.

Harless looked up at her. "Halloween, you mean?"

"Yeah. Folks in Toledo come out like this, you figure? You think it's such a big thing up there?"

Harless shrugged. He still had a toothpick in his mouth from Goffs', and it made him look like some kind of cowboy. "Maybe bigger, I don't know. Never been there on Halloween."

"But you've been to Ohio?"

"Rode through it once. Rode clear over to Illinois with my uncle—he drives a semi. Can sure see a lot of country from a seat in one of those."

"What's it look like? Ohio."

"Well, we headed out at night, so I didn't see anything till we reached the turnpike. Flat. You never saw land so flat—Ohio, Indiana, Illinois—even worse the farther you go, they say. You get out there in Iowa . . . Kansas . . . you don't see a hill anywhere. Not even a curve in the road, hardly. Land and corn and sky. That's what my uncle says. See a house or a tree, you get so excited you almost fall out the window."

A group of young teenagers dressed as rock musicians slunk and strutted up the hill toward the firehouse. Beth and Harless watched them, bemused.

"How about you?" Harless asked Beth. "How far you been from Crandall?"

"Hawk's Nest."

"That all? Where you *like* to go?"

"I don't hardly know." Beth looked down at his orange hair. "Seems like everyone who leaves never comes back, leastways not to stay. Mrs. Maxwell's sons left—one to Ohio and one to Pennsylvania. Sort of spooky when you think about it, like they'd all jumped off the edge of the earth."

"You ever think of leaving?"

"Do you?"

"Nope. Wouldn't want to live anywhere I couldn't look out my window and see hills. You leave the Appalachians, you've either got to go to Vermont or you've got to go clear out West to see any mountains. So I aim to settle right here."

"Doing what?"

"Whatever I can get. I like the delivery business. Don't have anybody looking over my shoulder all the time. Be my own boss."

"Did you graduate?"

"Nope. Got two years of high school, figured that was enough. Long as I got a truck, I can find work. You figure on staying in Crandall?"

"Sometimes yes, sometimes no."

It was curious talking to someone who had his back to her, Beth was thinking. It was easy, somehow, to sit up here on the seat of his truck and talk into the shadows. She could tell when he was smiling simply by the way his ears seemed to lower and his cheeks puff out. Could tell when he was serious by the way the sides of his face grew thinner. The trick to talking easy with boys, she decided, was to be someplace you didn't have to look at each other all the time, where you both had your eyes on something else. She'd remember to tell that to Geraldine. Clarice, even. In case they ever wanted to know.

Nine-thirty came sooner than Beth wanted it to, and she was surprised to see her brothers and sisters crossing the street by Kroger's, Lyle in the lead, swinging Shirley's cat's tail like a lasso.

They tumbled in the back of the pickup with their half-filled sacks and pillow cases, all chattering, teasing each other, noting the places they wanted to come again next year. Shirley crawled once more into Beth's lap, so tired she could scarcely hold her head up.

When Harless crossed the bridge and parked at last outside the Herndons' trailer, Beth was pleased to see that every one of her brothers and sisters stopped to thank him before running on inside. Beth climbed down with Douglas.

"You want to come in for a cup of coffee or something?" she asked. "Ma usually keeps a pot on."

"Naw, just count heads, make sure I got you all home. Tell your dad I'll see him Monday."

"Okay." Beth boosted Douglas up a little higher on her shoulder. His lips blew small puffs of air against her neck as he slept. "Thanks a lot, Harless. Really nice of you to give up your evening and do something like this."

"Nothing much else to do," he told her, and it was the only thing all evening he'd said that she wished he'd said differently.

She walked slowly toward the porch with Douglas, Shirley holding on to the pocket of her jacket, and started up the steps where Ruth Marie was waiting at the screen. The pickup backed, moved out onto the pavement, and then—with a short toot of the horn and a blink of the lights—it went down Shadbush Road again toward Crandall.

4

Beth had just lain down and turned out the light when she heard a car stop outside, footsteps on the ground, the slam of a screen door, and then voices in the main room. Mother's. Geraldine's. Then Mother's again. The footsteps were coming down the hall now, and suddenly Gerry dived into bed, all her clothes on, pulling the covers up over her head and giggling.

Beth giggled, too, and poked at her. "What've *you* been up to?"

More giggling.

Sticking her head under the covers, the way they did when they didn't want their voices to carry to their parents' bedroom, Beth asked, "What's got into you? Oh, Lordy! You sure smell of lard. Going to get it all over the sheets, you're not careful."

She reached for her three-ring notebook and propped it

under the covers, making a tent of the blankets, then brought the flashlight under, too, and turned it on.

Geraldine lay panting, the giggling having worked itself out. Her spiked green hair had fallen over and lay raggedly along one side of her face, and her mascara had smeared. "I had the *best* time!" she said. "Mother's 'bout to have a fit, though. Says I look loose."

Beth studied her and then they both burst out laughing again, grabbing at their pillows and holding them over their mouths. The notebook fell over, and Beth propped it up again.

"Loose hinges, that's what you've got. Look like you're about to fall apart, Gerry, I swear it."

"I had a *wonderful* time," her sister repeated.

"Jack Carey?"

"Umm-hm."

"How'd he stand the smell?"

"He had lard on his hair, too," Geraldine said, and laughed.

"You two spend the whole time kissing?"

"Just half. Oh, they had the best music! Everybody was dancing, even the firemen. Had doughnuts, too, and cider. Clarice and Joan were there—all kinds of people. Beth, I *wish* you'd have come! You tell Dad you're going next year for sure. Tell him in July, he wants advance notice."

"Well, the evening could have been worse," Beth said.

"I don't see how."

"Harless being nice had something to do with it."

The bed squeaked as Geraldine sat up on one elbow, pulling covers with her. "Harless Prather?"

"Yes."

"Some old man?"

"Twenty-two."

"Harless Prather? Twenty-*two*?"

"Shhhh."

"What's he like?"

"Nice, I told you. He even took us to Goffs' Restaurant to eat. Anything we wanted."

Gerry gasped. "He's *sweet* on you, Beth!"

"Didn't say he took just me, did I? Took us all."

"He wouldn't have done it if you weren't riding up there in the front seat beside him. He touch you?"

"No! Think I'm going to throw myself at a boy just because he looks at me?"

"He *looked* at you then." Geraldine was grinning. Beth started grinning, too. They laughed aloud, then shushed each other.

"What's he look like?" Geraldine whispered.

"Nice looking. Real fine white teeth. Best teeth I ever saw. He's tall. Skinny like me. Orange hair the color of cooked carrots."

Geraldine's eyes grew larger. "I *saw* him then. He came to the party around ten. Sitting over there with the firemen talking. That *had* to be him. String-bean skinny and hair like orange peel."

Beth felt her chest going flat, as though the air were seeping out a hole in her lungs, and her pleasure in the evening along with it.

"He with somebody?"

"I don't think so. Seemed awful shy. Some girls got him

out on the floor dancing, but his face got as red as his hair, and then he went back and sat with the firemen again."

Beth lay without moving. Harless *had* been eager to leave then, and she couldn't blame him. She remembered now the way he'd asked the others to be back at the truck by nine-thirty. He'd wanted to get to that party by ten. And he hadn't asked Beth if she wanted to go with him, either. Probably going to meet someone.

"He's not interested in me," she said aloud. "Old enough to be a fireman himself. Old enough to be married, even. Twenty-two's a whole *lot* of years older than fifteen."

"Dad's eight years older than Ma," Geraldine reminded her.

"Did I say I was marrying him? Did I say he'd asked? Did I say I was even sweet on him?"

"Shhhh. Dad'll hear."

"Well, just hush up about Harless. He was nice to us, and that's all there is to the story. All I said was the evening could have been worse. All in the world I said!"

"Okay, okay." Geraldine got out of bed and groped around in the dark for the T-shirt she slept in, then went down the narrow hall to the bathroom.

Beth removed the flashlight and notebook from under the covers and set them on the floor, then turned and faced the wall.

She concentrated hard on her evening prayers. She had taken to praying sometime around her twelfth birthday, but wasn't sure exactly why. It had just felt as though, being the first one of the Herndon children to start junior high school, she'd needed someone along, and when she couldn't seem to find a time her mother could talk with her, or the right words to use with her father, talking to Jesus came easy.

She wasn't even sure she was doing it right. The Herndons did not pray aloud at mealtimes, but that didn't mean they weren't religious. There was an old Bible on the magazine stand near the sofa, and Beth often found her mother reading it first thing in the morning while she had her coffee. Beth would come out to make her own breakfast, and Mother would have one finger on a Bible verse, following it along the page, her lips moving silently as she read.

They did not go to church most Sundays, either, because Mother cleaned rooms at Goffs' seven days a week, and it was Wednesdays, not Sundays, Dad had off at the diner. But sometimes, if there was a special service on Christmas or Thanksgiving and the diner was closed, Ray and Lorna Herndon gathered up their children, saw that their clothes were pressed, and piled them all in the pickup. Church twice a year was fifty short of church every Sunday, however, so Beth had her own way of praying.

Dear Lord Jesus and God, she said this time, silently to herself, *it's probably a good thing Gerry told me about Harless Prather being at the party because I can see myself being the fool over him and an everlasting disgrace. Thank you for our belongings and our home and the food to put on the table. And protect Gerry when she doesn't have enough sense to see straight, which is a whole lot of the time lately. Amen.*

It seemed unfinished somehow—as though there were something more she wanted or needed to ask, but Beth couldn't think of anything she didn't have that she couldn't do without, and it seemed to her that if you asked Jesus for every little thing, he might not answer when the really important needs rolled around. So she held off.

In English the following Monday, the teacher gave the class most of the period to write first drafts of their themes. It wasn't the writing of it that bothered Beth—not the thoughts, anyway. Thoughts tumbled out of her head like salt from a shaker. It was the way she had to write them. In this case, the theme paper about her career goals was to include every type of clause there was in English grammar. Clarice had been right.

Beth's head swam. Restrictive clauses, nonrestrictive clauses, independent and dependent clauses, subordinate clauses . . . Clauses, as far as she could figure out, were simply bunches of words between commas, and she determined where commas themselves should go by reading aloud what she had written and noting where her voice hesitated naturally. Then she stuck in a comma.

She leaned her head in her hand and watched Miss Wentworth—beautiful Miss Wentworth—silently listing on the board all the things that they should pay attention to in their theme papers: spelling, capitalization, punctuation, clarity, unity . . .

Beth could not figure out either Miss Wentworth or Miss Talbot—the only two teachers in the school she envied. Miss Wentworth was shorter than the typing teacher, but with her brains and her thick, dark hair and eyelashes, she could probably do and be anything at all. What on earth attracted her to clauses? And why did Miss Talbot stay here in Crandall when she could have been modeling clothes on the cover of *Vogue* magazine?

Miss Wentworth turned from the blackboard and walked softly back toward her desk, eyes scanning the classroom as students bent over their papers, pens scribbling. Her eyes lit on Beth, and her eyebrows raised quizzically. Beth hurriedly picked up her pen and read over what she had written so far:

What I Want to Do with the Rest of My Life

Beth Herndon, English 102

It's easier to say what I don't want to do, which is end up without any kind of job I really like. Even if I get maried. I see lots of people go to work every day and don't even like it. I think women should all *be* something before they marry.

I'm very good at things with my hands. I'm very good at typing and I would like to be a typist with a fine company. I think I could be really happy in a job where I had my own desk and nice people to work with and stacks of things to type. I could type all day long and never get tired.

Beth sighed. She hardly had any commas at all! She crossed out the two paragraphs and tried again.

What I Want to Do with the Rest of My Life

Beth Herndon, English 102

It's easier to say what I don't want to do, which is spend the rest of my life doing what I've done already,

64

taking care of babies. I want to have a job I really like, even if I get maried. I think women should all *be* something before they marry and have a lot of children, so they can do it again when the children are groan.

I'm very good at doing things with my hands, my fingers, really. My best subject in school is typing, and I would like to become a typist with a good company. I think I could be really happy in a job where I had my own desk and nice people to work with and stacks and stacks of things to type. I could type all day long and never get tired one bit, I got fingers like wings. They just fly. . . .

She caught Clarice's eye in the next row, and they exchanged pained glances. English wasn't Clarice's best subject, either, but she was good at it, better than Beth. School was easier for Clarice, probably because her dad was a dentist—somebody who had finished school himself.

Beth made little dots along the margin of her paper as she tried to think what to write next. Her mind wandered, however. Clarice had seen Harless Prather at the party, too. She had mentioned him that morning. Not even knowing that Harless had taken Beth and her brothers and sisters around on Halloween, she'd told how there was this tall, shy boy with orange hair that Joan, her sister, had coaxed to dance.

"He take her home after?" Beth had asked casually.

"No. Joan had her own car. I don't know who the guy was, but Joan thought he was cute. You even look at him, though, he blushes."

Well, that made two of them then—she and Harless were

both blushers. Grinners and blushers. Probably the only two things they had in common.

Beth had said no more. Didn't want it known that she'd been in Harless Prather's truck, didn't want anyone getting the idea that she liked him and then telling her he was someone else's boyfriend.

The weather turned sharply colder in November, and Beth's old jacket, too short in the sleeves, was no longer warm enough, as Mother predicted.

"Beth, the wind'll go right through that cloth," Lorna Herndon said one morning when the windows had steamed up so badly that Beth had to wipe them off to see if the bus was coming. "Saw some coats on sale at the Super Dollar. You do one more batch of flowers for Mrs. Goff, I think you got the money to buy one."

"Then I've got to do them myself," Beth said. "No fair me keeping all the money if you're helping."

"Well, if you figure you can handle it."

The coat was warm, lined with acrylic pile, and had a collar that could be turned up, and a matching scarf in green and blue. Beth dressed carefully the first day she wore it, liking the feel of her long hair tucked securely down inside the collar, the wrap of the scarf about her neck. She even found herself smiling as she stepped into the bus.

"Pretty coat, Beth," Mrs. Shayhan said when Beth slipped into the seat behind her.

"Thanks," Beth said, still smiling. Grinning, she discovered. *Dear Lord Jesus and God, help me to take happiness*

66

without spreading it clear across my face. Sure sign of being young, she thought.

Beth had no close friends on the bus. If anyone said more than hi to her, it was usually Mrs. Shayhan. Everyone else came from neighborhoods where they knew at least two or three others on their street. But being out here between the cliff and the river, far removed from the trailer court, even, Beth made friends mostly with those she met in her classes, who socialized with her at lunchtime, talked with her in gym, then went their separate ways when school was out. Close as she felt to Clarice, in fact, Beth had never been to her house; wasn't even sure where she lived. The other side of Crandall, most certainly.

The only person on the bus who was in one of Beth's classes was Stephanie King, and Stephanie usually sat at the back. This bus picked up students first from the Belcrest section—the new houses back on Taylor Drive where Stephanie lived. Then it worked its way over to Shadbush Road, the final stretch, before turning around again at the falls, heading back, and crossing the bridge into Crandall.

Beth tried occasionally to catch Stephanie's eye when she got on—wanted, really, to make friends if she could. This feud, if that's what it was, that had sprung up between them in typing was the silliest thing. Of course Beth liked to get the top grade. Of course she was disappointed when the honor went to Stephanie. But it was more like a race, a game—to her, anyway. Nothing to get mad over. Yet she knew if she ever said that to Stephanie, the blond-haired girl would look at her with wide, blue eyes and say, "Who's mad?" She'd smile and act as though Beth had said the dumbest thing in the world, but the next time Beth got the top grade in typing, Stephanie, as usual, would look the other way.

It was Beth's grin that did it—that widemouthed grin she couldn't control—and the more Beth tried to hide it, the broader it grew; the more she tried not to look at Stephanie as she passed with her test paper, the more determinedly her eyes—with a mind of their own, it seemed—sought her out. Stephanie must have thought Beth was jeering at her and, quite naturally, always turned away. It had become a routine of sorts: the grade, the grin, the look, the turn. And so, when Beth got on the bus in her new coat and looked toward Stephanie, Stephanie began talking with the boy beside her, ignoring Beth altogether.

Beth had no illusions that her new coat would bring her popularity, good grades, and romance, but she had hoped for a little more than the day produced.

Miss Wentworth had a lot to say about Beth's theme paper, for one thing, most of it bad. As the rest of the class worked on an assignment about prepositions, the teacher called each student privately up to her desk to discuss the drafts of their themes they'd turned in two days before. When Beth sat down by Miss Wentworth's desk, enveloped in the most exquisite perfume, the paper the teacher was holding had so many red marks on it, it looked like chicken pox.

Miss Wentworth gave a wry smile. "Well, we've got a lot of work to do on this, Beth," she said, running one beautifully manicured hand—the hand with the diamond engagement ring on it—through her hair. "I have no trouble at all with the thoughts you express; it's the way you express them. I also see a lot of commas on the page, but you were to indicate in the margins wherever you used a clause, and label which kind it was. Remember? Read through the chapter on clauses again and label your second draft. Spelling is giving you a problem, too, I can see, so keep a dictionary handy. You also need to watch your syntax. This sentence, for example: 'I think women should all *be* something before they marry and have a lot of children, so they can do it again when the children are grown.' Do what again?"

She turned to Beth, and suddenly Beth felt her cheeks blaze, then turn even pinker as the teacher, flustered, began to blush, too.

"*You* know, and *I* know, that you are referring to work —something they can go back to after their children are grown—but the way you've written it, it's ambiguous. Because in the first part of the sentence you're referring to the women's *being* something, and in the last part you refer to their *doing* something. You see?"

They were all words to Beth, nothing but words. If *she* knew what she was talking about and the *teacher* knew, then what was the problem? There was something embarrassing about the way it sounded, however. Beth nodded silently and waited while Miss Wentworth pointed out a place where a semicolon should have been used instead of a comma, a comma instead of a period, a period where there wasn't any punctuation at all.

Miss Wentworth started to hand the paper back, then studied it a moment longer and said, "I like your final paragraph,

Beth. I like it very much." She smiled and Beth took the paper back to her seat as another student was called to the teacher's desk.

While pens around her scribbled, feet shuffled, and chairs squeaked, Beth silently read her final paragraph. After writing about the kind of job she would like to have, the salary she hoped to achieve, and the family she wanted to start someday, Beth had written:

> The only real questin in my mind is not can I do it, because I think I can, but do I want to stay here? Somebody told me he's seen a lot of other states flat as cow patties, not a hill anywhere. I can't imagin living where the land is flat, but it seems to me that until you've been somewhere, you've always got this itch to go see for yourself. Trouble is, lots of people leave Crandall and never come back no matter how ugly it is where they've gone. I think I'd like to see what's outside West Virginia, too, but maybe I'll be one of the ones who comes back.

And in the margin, in red pencil, Miss Wentworth had written, "I hope so."

That little note in the margin was about the only nice thing that happened in school, because Stephanie King got one point higher than Beth on the typing test, and in biology, Beth was horrified when all the students were paired off and handed a preserved frog in a plastic bag to dissect. They had to find the heart, the lungs, and the liver. Beth's partner was a large boy with clumsy hands who insisted all through the procedure that he was about to vomit.

Beth told Mrs. Shayhan about it on the bus going home, and the driver laughed. "Well, I'm glad I left school before my sophomore year, then, because if somebody handed me a dead frog in a plastic bag, that's the last they'd see of me, I can tell you." Her laughter filled the bus. "Haven't met one person in my entire life who ever needed to know how to cut up a dead frog. Why don't they teach you kids how to lay kitchen tile or put in a new pane of glass? That's what I'd like to know."

Beth smiled as she stepped off the bus and crossed the road. Just wearing her new coat gave her a lift, and talking with Mrs. Shayhan gave her another. Inside the house, she stood in front of the mirror on the bathroom door and admired the coat again before she took it off.

"Looks real nice," her mother said, noticing. "Green's a good color on you, Beth." She was doing another basket of ironing for Mrs. Goff.

"You tired? Look tired," Beth commented.

"Got another basket to do after this one," Lorna said. "My back's been hurting me some."

"You sit down and I'll iron awhile," Beth told her, taking over, and Mother gave no argument.

The family returned to home base in shifts again—three, then two, then one as Father came in the door. Beth continued ironing as her dad poured himself a glass of milk and drank it leaning against the wall, talking to Lorna above the blare of the TV.

"George Dean sure did jump all over Harless when he come by with the rolls today. Said it's the last batch of rolls half burned on the bottom that he's going to take."

"I should guess so," said Mother.

"Harless says we'll get credit on the bill, but that they've been having a problem with their oven. George says, 'Well, you got a problem with your oven, you got to have it fixed, because *I* got problems with my customers!' "

Beth waited, pressing the iron down on a pillowcase. It was the first time since Halloween that her father had mentioned Harless Prather, and she tried not to seem interested.

"Not Harless's fault, though," Ray Herndon continued, "and he sure does get embarrassed, you talk to him that way. Face turns red as a brake light. He gets along fine with folks younger than he is, but don't know quite how to handle George Dean. Like he says, all he does is deliver, but he get a lot of dissatisfied buyers, he won't have nobody to deliver to."

Beth turned the pillowcase over and ironed the other side, then folded it into thirds and ironed it still again. Her father raised his voice so he could be heard around the room.

"Harless wanted to know if any of you kids got sick from all that candy."

"I didn't!" sang out Shirley.

"Not me," said Bud.

"Said I had a nice family," Dad continued. He set his glass down on the dinette table and walked over to the sofa, sinking down beside Mother, taking off his shoes and tossing them into one corner. The smaller children slid off the couch to make room and sat on the floor instead, leaning back against their parents' knees.

Beth had just placed the folded pillowcase with the rest and picked up another when her father said, "Harless wanted to know how old you were, Beth. Said he couldn't believe you was fifteen."

Beth's hand paused on the iron, then moved jerkily so as not to scorch the cloth. "Why not?" she asked.

Her father chuckled a little. "Thought you were an old lady, maybe, I don't know. Said you sure made the kids behave."

Beth tried to decipher the words. Was that a compliment? Or was Harless saying she was too stiff, too bossy? Had she smiled enough? Had she, in fact, laughed at all the entire evening, let him know she'd enjoyed herself—all the money he'd spent on them? She tried desperately to remember.

"You never told us if you had a good time or not," Mother put in, looking in Beth's direction.

"It was okay," Beth said. Then, mindful that her father might repeat it to Harless word for word, she added, "He was nice."

"Well, that's what Harless said about you," said Ray, eyes smiling.

Beth found herself racing the iron over the next pillowcase and the next. Her father was absolutely maddening. She wanted to know everything. What her father had said. What Harless had said. Exactly. Word for word. How his voice sounded when he said it, how his face had looked. Had he smiled? Had he laughed? Was it a polite sort of laugh, or did his eyes crinkle, like he was teasing, like he maybe really liked her? How had her name come up? Did he just get out of his truck and say, "Mr. Herndon, how old is Beth?" Or did he sort of lead up to it first? If Clarice had been there, she'd have recorded everything in her head like a movie.

Harless and Beth. Beth and Harless. It was the first time Beth had put the names together, and she liked the sound of them. The weeks and months ahead came rolling toward her. Thanksgiving, Christmas . . . *Beth and Harless in the snow.* Spring. *Beth and Harless on the grass.* Summer, with Beth and Harless riding around in his pickup truck, the windows open, radio going—driving right up to the Dairy Bar, laughing.

She checked herself suddenly as she realized she'd written the ending before Harless had even gotten a foot in the story. Still, all through supper, the thought of Harless Prather came back again—the only boy who had ever driven her somewhere, and he wasn't put off by all the kids. Her father was kind that night, too, smiling and joking with her at the table. If ever once she could just figure out what she did that made him warm toward her and what she did that made him cold . . . !

It was after the meal was over, when Ray Herndon had gone bowling and Douglas and Shirley had been put to bed, that Beth went into her parents' bedroom to help Mother sort through some clothes in her closet.

"I got blouses there never did seem to fit right, and they hang from one month to the next," Lorna told her. "You don't want any of 'em, I'll give 'em to Mrs. Maxwell. No sense even trying them out on Geraldine. Gerry don't wear nothing unless it looks like somethin' you'd use to mop the floor."

Beth laughed and so did her mother. Reaching into the

74

back of the closet, Mother took out a red jersey top and handed it to Beth, watching while she tried it on.

"Red looks good on you. Brings out the pink in your cheeks. You like that one, you can have it." Mother took several more shirts from the closet and laid them on the bed for Beth, then stretched her arms high and took down a box from the top shelf. "Might as well tell you now as later, Beth, but I'm expecting a baby next May sometime."

Beth stood absolutely motionless. "You are, Ma?" Her voice hardly seemed to have strength enough to say the words.

Mrs. Herndon set the box on the bed, smiling a little. "Don't know the date exactly, but I got all the signs, and May's as close as I can figure. Thought we might as well sort through some baby clothes while we're at it, see what the moths have got."

Beth stared at her mother, at the thin figure standing beside the bed, taking out baby things one by one. Slowly Beth took off the red blouse and reached for her own shirt again. *Nine* children? There were going to be nine in this family now, in this double-wide trailer that was already filled to overflowing? There was going to be another baby next May when Harless came to call for her in his pickup? Just when she'd thought she could get away sometimes, go riding around Crandall like the other kids did, there would be another baby to bottle, bathe, and diaper?

Mechanically she buttoned her shirt, her heart pounding, unmindful of the other things waiting to be tried on. And suddenly, because she knew it was the best chance she'd ever have, she said, "Ma, the nurse at school—she said maybe you'd like to talk to a clinic."

Lorna Herndon's back stiffened and she looked at Beth strangely.

"What's she know about me? I got a midwife to come, same as for all of you. Don't need a clinic."

Beth's voice was hesitant. "No, I mean . . . she said there's something you could do . . . to stop getting pregnant so much. . . ."

The slap landed on her cheek before Beth ever saw the hand coming. The hurt, white look on her mother's face, the blur of the hand, the sound of the slap, the sting of fingers against her cheek . . .

They faced each other awkwardly.

"Ma . . . !"

"Don't you never let me hear that kind of talk again." Lorna's voice was thick, husky. "You talking to a school nurse about nobody's business but mine."

Beth felt a flash of anger along with the sting and the embarrassment. "All she did was ask how many kids in the family, and all I did was answer. That's when she told me."

"Well, she didn't have no right asking and you no business telling. No business at all talking about things like that. How many children I have is for me to decide, and what a woman does not to have them is something you don't need to know a thing about."

Beth struggled desperately to keep her anger in check. She had to make her mother understand.

"I'm worried about you, Ma. You're tired enough already. If there was some simple thing you could do to stop having babies . . ."

Lorna Herndon's voice was shrill. "I'd done somethin' before to keep from having children, some of you wouldn't be here. You ever think of that? Who you figure I could have done without, Beth? You? Lyle? Betty Jo? Shirley? Who you want to send back?"

"Ma, I didn't mean . . ."

"Here's the way I look at it, Elizabeth Pearl. Children are my blessings, and as long as the good Lord keeps sending them, I'll keep having them." Angrily she overturned the box on the bed, and an odd assortment of baby clothes spilled out—faded sweaters, little stained shirts, bibs, booties . . .

Beth fled the room, ignoring the stares of Geraldine and the others, grabbed her coat, and went out. The wind blew hard against her face. She thrust her bare hands in her pockets and followed the rocky cliff along the road in darkness for a quarter mile until the base of the rock swerved in again under an overhang. Into this "cave" Beth crawled, hoisting herself up on ledges of rock until she was sheltered on three sides from the wind. She found the large, flat boulder near the back where they had often played "church" or "school"—the boulder becoming either the preacher's pulpit or the teacher's desk—and there she sat.

As long as the good Lord keeps sending them. Forever, then. Her mother was only thirty-two. There was another baby coming after Douglas, and probably others after that—a long procession of feedings, and two or three children to a bed. Only the week before, Mother had said something vague about the possibility of Ruth Marie sleeping on a cot in Beth and Geraldine's room, and Beth should have got the message then. Mother was already figuring out how she could squeeze one more child into the household, bedrooms not much bigger than closets.

By the spring of her sophomore year, then, there would be nine children—eleven people altogether—in a trailer meant for six, eight at the most. It seemed to Beth as though the story of her life had already been written, and she would have no say in it. All she had to do was get up in the morning, go onstage, and some unseen director would move her about from class to class, drive her around with Harless, and home again. What would be would be.

She sat shivering on the rock, her fingers clutched into fists inside her pockets. The only way to fit another person in the front door was to let one go out the back, and maybe she would be the first to leave.

5

Beth knew that Harless would come. It was the same kind of certainty as geese flying south for the winter, and when she heard the sound of a truck stopping outside the house on Friday evening, she put down the dish towel, went in the bathroom to brush her teeth, and heard Lyle answer the door.

"Hey, Harless! Come on in!"

Footsteps, cries of greeting from Bud and Shirley.

"How you doin'?" Harless's voice.

"What's the matter, Prather? You make a delivery and get lost?" Dad's voice. Joking.

Harless laughed, too, and Beth was amazed at how familiar it sounded, as though she'd known this man a long time. "Just driving around. Thought I'd come by, see what Beth's doing."

"*I'll* drive around with you!" Bud offered.

"Sometime, but not tonight," Harless told him, and Beth's heart pounded even harder as she rinsed her mouth.

Then Geraldine's voice. "I'll get Beth," and her footsteps sounded on the floor outside the bathroom.

She poked her head in. "It's Harless!"

Beth smiled excitedly and edged down the hallway to their bedroom to change sweaters. Gerry followed, closing the door after them.

"He's so tall! Bet you hardly reach his shoulder, Beth!" She giggled.

Hurriedly Beth yanked off her gray sweater and put on her blue one. "What have I got to reach him for?" she asked, and this time they both giggled.

"Where you two going?" Gerry wanted to know.

"Didn't say he was taking me anywhere, did he?"

With a quick sweep of the brush through her hair, Beth walked back out to the front room. Harless was hand-wrestling with Bud over by the door and had Bud's arm pinned behind his back. Bud was yelping and laughing both at the same time.

"Hold on, here," Harless told him when he saw Beth, and let go. His face broke into a wide grin. "Was just riding by, wondered if you were needing to go anywhere—drugstore or something—I could take you."

"Nowhere in particular," Beth said, not knowing how else to answer.

"You two looking for an errand, you could pick me up some navy blue thread," Lorna said from her seat at the dinette table where she was shortening an old skirt of Ruth Marie's for Betty Jo.

"You want to go get some thread?" Harless asked Beth, smiling a little foolishly, face coloring.

"Takes two people and a truck to go get a fifty-cent spool?" Beth replied, smiling back.

"Thread sure comes heavy these days," joked Harless.

Beth took her coat from the hook near the door and put one hand on the doorknob.

"Put some gloves on, girl, it's winter out there," her father told her. And then, to Harless, "Hasn't got the sense of a polecat."

Beth cast her father a quick, hurt glance, then grabbed her gloves and went out. Harless said his good-byes, then clattered down the steps after her.

"He always after you that way?"

"Most always."

"He don't mean nothing by it," Harless told her, opening the truck door, and Beth climbed up.

"Sure could have fooled me," she said.

Harless walked around the truck and jumped in, resting his hands on his thighs. "Now where you want to go?"

Beth laughed at him then. "You're the one had the idea to come over. Where do *you* want to go?"

He snapped his fingers. "Got to get that thread," he said, turning the key in the ignition, and they headed toward Crandall.

Harless had a good smell about him—like Old Spice cologne, or maybe it was just Mum and shampoo. From time to time Beth stole a look at him, his profile against the moonlight that streamed through his window. He had thin, fine features like hers, but his lips were fuller, and his Adam's apple jutted out like a walnut from his neck. With one hand, he turned up the collar of his jacket.

"Heater's not workin' so good, but it'll warm up some in a few minutes," he said. "Got to get it fixed."

"I'm fine," Beth told him. And then, "So what were you doing way out here that you happened to be riding by?"

Though she could see only his silhouette, she could tell he was smiling.

"Went to see the falls."

Beth laughed out loud. "In pitch blackness?"

"There's a good moon out. Look."

"You went to see the falls in the moonlight all by yourself?"

"Couldn't get my mom to go," Harless said, and they both laughed. "I'll take *you*," he added, as though it just occurred to him. "*You* want to see the falls by moonlight?" He slowed as though ready to turn the truck around.

"No, go on," she giggled, and shoved his arm.

"The real reason," Harless said, "I was wondering what you was like without a kid in your lap and another between us here on the seat. Now that's the truth."

"Well, here I am," Beth retorted. "Not much different than when Shirley and Douglas were here."

"*Seem* different," he told her.

It was as easy to talk to Harless here in the truck as it was when he was standing outside it on Halloween, Beth thought. Maybe it was because it was dark and they didn't have to look at each other directly. Or maybe it was a whole lot easier to talk to a boy alone than she'd ever imagined. The fact that she was thinking about it now, however, made her self-conscious, and when a minute or two had gone by without any more said between them, Harless reached out and turned on the radio. It was always someone moaning about love, it seemed—a man, this time.

The music helped to fill the gap, however, and Beth leaned back against the seat as though intent on the song. She was thinking, actually, about her mother and the baby to come, and whether it would ruin all this—her going out with Harless.

They had said nothing more about the pregnancy, she and Mother, since the night of the slap in the bedroom. The embarrassment of it was worse than the hurt, and they'd each gone about their tasks silently. How much Betty Jo and the others had heard, Beth didn't know. But when she'd told Geraldine that Mother was expecting again, Gerry said simply, "I figured so." There wasn't much else to say.

Suddenly the singer's words intruded:

> *. . . Then what I hope and what I dream,*
> *Is that your lips be kind;*
> *Your arms so tightly 'round my neck,*
> *Your body next to mine.*

"We could maybe try the Super Dollar," Beth said quickly, and Harless was already reaching for the dial, turning the volume down. "Most anywhere that's open carries thread."

It was a strange feeling walking into the Super Dollar beside Harless Prather. Gerry was right; Beth's head just came to his shoulder, maybe an inch or so above it, and he seemed to tower over her as they walked down the aisle toward the notions department. Beth both wanted and didn't want to be

83

seen. If she had to introduce him to somebody, what would she call him? Could you even say, "This is my friend, Harless," when you'd only seen him twice in your life?

It was one of those times when things seemed to work out perfectly. The only person Beth knew who saw her in the store was Stephanie King, shopping with her mother, and since Stephanie had developed the habit of looking the other way when Beth glanced at her, Beth felt no obligation to introduce Harless at all. But all the while she was comparing shades of navy blue, holding up one spool against a spool Harless had in his hand, Beth could feel Stephanie's eyes on her from two counters away, and Beth's grin, as usual, took over her whole face. Maybe it *was* deliberate. Maybe she *did* take joy in letting Stephanie King, honor student, know that somebody out on Shadbush Road had something going for her, too.

"You figure your ma needs this thread right away, or could we go somewhere first?" Harless said as they went back outside, the package in Beth's hand.

"She won't need it right this second," Beth told him.

"If I hadn't come by, she wouldn't have it at all, right?"

"Right."

"So you want to go get something to eat, see the falls by moonlight?"

Beth didn't know how to answer. What did it mean when a boy asked you to do that? What were you agreeing to do? Harless seemed to sense her discomfort because he said quickly, "Okay, one at a time. You want something to eat?"

"Don't you ever eat at home?" She laughed.

"Ever' chance I get," he said. "I'm a growing boy. Figure I still got another couple inches to go."

Beth smiled. "All right."

They went to the drive-in, and Beth enjoyed sitting high in the pickup, waited on at the window. She ordered a chocolate shake while Harless ordered a cheeseburger, fries, and a hot apple pie. He took the tray inside when the girl brought it, to keep the heat in the truck.

"Can't understand why you don't get fat, all you put away," Beth told him, crossing her legs and wiggling one foot to the music on the radio.

"I work it off," he said.

"Just driving around making deliveries?"

"Play basketball a lot with my brothers. Always a bunch of fellas over at the school yard ready to play."

"Are your brothers older or younger?"

"I'm the oldest."

"Same with me."

"That's what I figured. So we got something in common on that score." Harless took a bite, concentrating on his chewing, and Beth slowly sipped her shake.

She watched the activity in the lot—cars pulling in and out; the girl in the red cap, shoulders hunched against the wind, running over to take their orders. . . . The thing about going out with boys, she decided, the thing that made it interesting and scary both, was that you never knew what would happen next.

"What else do you do in your spare time?" she asked finally.

Harless chewed a bit longer, then swallowed. "That's about all the spare time I got. Delivery job takes nine hours a day. I play a little basketball, eat, sleep, and whatever time's left over, Dad's got work for me to do around the place, or the truck needs fixing." He glanced over at her. "What about you? What all you do besides go to school and take care of babies?"

"That's about it."

"No boyfriend?" And before Beth could answer, he said, "Besides me, I mean."

She felt the color rising in her cheeks and hoped he couldn't see it in the semidarkness. "You're sure talking big," she said.

"Sorry."

Then she felt bad that she'd said it. "I mean . . ." She looked at him and smiled. "No other boyfriend." Her pulse raced.

And, just like that, Harless stretched one arm across the back of the seat, letting his fingers touch her shoulder, ever so lightly—the softest little touch. The music played on, and Beth finished her shake, relishing the warmth of his fingers through her coat, heady with the thrill of being here with him like this.

When they were through eating, Harless blinked the lights and the girl in the red cap came over and took their tray. He started the engine and pulled out.

Beth's heart beat a hard, frantic rhythm as they headed toward Shadbush Road again. The falls? Maybe she'd been too forward, saying what she did. Maybe things were moving along too fast.

"I think maybe I ought to get this thread back home to

Ma," she said. She glanced over at him, wondering if she'd hurt his feelings, calling an end to the evening like this after they'd had a nice time.

"It's okay, the falls can wait," he said.

And when he got her home, he hopped out, came around to open the door for her, and helped her down. Once her hand was in his, however, he didn't let go right away. Just stood there looking down at her, his hair shiny orange around the edges where it caught the light from the house. One thumb gently caressed her palm.

"Good-night, Beth."

"Good-night. And thanks a lot."

He let her go. Didn't even try to kiss her. Beth didn't know if she was sorry or not. But as she reached the steps, he called out something.

"What?" she said, turning.

"Sure wish you had a phone."

"Be a hot day in January that ever happens," she said, laughing, and went in.

Once inside, it seemed as though everyone was looking at her.

"I look dead or something, you all staring?" she asked. And then, to her mother, "Here's your thread." She laid it on the dinette table and took off her coat. Her father watched her without comment, and after she'd taken an apple from the refrigerator, Beth sauntered on back to the bedroom. Geraldine got up from the couch and followed her in.

"What'd you do? What's he like?" Gerry asked, closing the door.

Beth took a bite of apple and plopped down on the bed. "What happened was we went to the Super Dollar for thread and then the drive-in where I watched him eat a whole supper. That's about all the excitement I could stand for one evening, so he brought me home."

"But what *happened*?"

Beth leaned back against the wall, grinning. "He asked if I had any other boyfriends besides him."

"Really? He asked that?"

Beth nodded, the grin growing wider.

"What did you say?"

"I said, 'No other boyfriends.' "

"Then you're *going* with him!" Geraldine said breathlessly.

"I didn't ask if he had any other *girl*friends, though."

Geraldine thought that one over. "I don't think he'd be asking that kind of question if he didn't want you asking him in return."

"Guess that's what I figured, too."

Gerry looked at her cautiously. "He kiss you?"

"No."

"Try to?"

"No."

"He *didn't*?"

"Gerry, hush up! I ask you how you spend the least little second with Jack Carey?"

"Just curious is all."

"Well, no charge for being curious." Beth grinned again and went on eating the apple, wiggling her feet.

That night, after she had gone to bed—Gerry staying up

late at the dinette table to do an assignment—Beth heard the noises from her parents' room, the love noises.

She rolled over on her stomach, pulling both pillows close to her ears, shutting out the sounds. It hardly seemed fair that she and Geraldine had to listen, not being married themselves. It made her think of what it would be like to sit in Harless Prather's truck at the falls; Harless's touch—the warmth of his fingers there on her shoulders, the way his thumb had caressed her hand. *Your arms so tightly 'round my neck, your body next to mine.*

Riding into school on Monday, Beth prayed her first prayer in a week. It seemed important, somehow, before she and Harless saw each other again. To be truthful, she hadn't wanted to talk to the Lord since finding out that her mother was pregnant. If God was sending the blessings, she wasn't at all sure she had anything to say to him.

Help me learn about Harless and when to say no, she prayed silently, watching the glint of the morning sun glaze the top of the water. She figured that whatever she had left unsaid, the Savior could figure it out, he being a man himself. But she couldn't help adding a P.S.: *Please, dear Jesus and God, after this one, don't send us any more blessings. We've got enough.*

In the cafeteria at noon, she decided to tell Clarice about Harless Prather. Clarice turned and faced her with her mouth wide open, a crumb from her sandwich still stuck to her lip.

"Him?" she asked, wide-eyed, laying her sandwich down. Then, "Him!" she shrieked again, grabbing Beth's arm. "Oh,

Beth! The guy with the carrot top? The one who danced with *Joan*?" And just when Beth was positive that Clarice would tell her that Harless was really married, with babies, yet, Clarice gave a little squeal of delight, and Beth knew she was home free.

"Oh, Lordy, that's wonderful! Him! I never dreamed! Tell me everything! Start at the beginning!" Clarice was an even better audience than Gerry.

It was remarkable how you could exaggerate the details and string a story out, Beth thought as they sat on the wall outside in the sun after lunch, waiting for the bell. Beth explained about Halloween and eating at Goffs' and parking downtown by the savings and loan, and every time she stopped for breath, it was Clarice's cue to squeal.

"Why didn't you tell me *before*?"

"Didn't seem like there was much to tell. Till last night, anyway."

"Oh, Beth, it's so romantic! And he's *twenty-two*!"

The weekend was particularly balmy for November—as though autumn was giving the mountain state a final respite before the onslaught of winter snows. As soon as Dad got home from the diner that Saturday, he and Lyle and Mr. Maxwell went up the road with the chain saw to where the rocky wall gave way to earth, and then they climbed up the steep hill on county land, dragging the saw. Beth could imagine it almost every step of the way because she'd gone with them herself. They'd climb around through the leaves, looking for limbs that had fallen—whole trees, even—sawing the dead wood into pieces and rolling them down the hill toward the pickup. Then they'd stack them in the open back of the truck and drive around Crandall, looking for houses with fireplace chimneys, asking if any firewood was needed. Even now she could hear the distant sound of the chain saw while she hand-washed her gym clothes in the bathroom.

When she'd finished the washing, she took the vacuum cleaner to the bedrooms, then dusted the furniture—her Saturday jobs. All afternoon she expected Harless to come and take her somewhere, but it was getting on toward suppertime. She had curled the ends of her hair that morning and was wearing a cherry-red shirt with her jeans, just in case. After she put the vacuum cleaner back in the closet, she heard the sound of a motor and ran to the window.

There was a gray Honda in the space in front of the Maxwells' trailer, parked askew. Nobody seemed to be getting out, but Beth could see heads bobbing, faces peering out the windows. Then the driver turned around again, and Beth recognized Clarice.

She jumped back, not wanting to be seen. Clarice *here*? How did Clarice know where she lived? Then she realized that since Clarice worked in the school office an hour each morning, she knew where almost everybody lived. If Beth didn't go out, the girls would come to the door and knock, and the house smelled like dirty diapers. She ran outside.

Clarice had two other girls from school with her. They were laughing, and Clarice rolled down her window. "Surprise!"

Beth managed a smile, "What are *you* doing here?"

"I just got my driver's license!" Clarice said excitedly. "I told Daddy we were driving to the falls, and then I remembered you lived on Shadbush Road. We looked for your mailbox on the way back."

Beth could see the other girls—the one in front and the brunette in the backseat—stealing glances at the Herndons' trailer, their smiles too benevolent, faces too cheery.

"Didn't run over anybody yet," Clarice said, laughing. "Daddy's probably home having a stroke. I've got to get the car back, but just wanted to say hello."

"So hello," Beth joked.

"All this yours?" said the brunette, motioning toward the trailers. "It's so cozy."

"One's ours, one's the Maxwells'," Beth murmured. "Listen, I've got to get back inside. I'm cooking dinner."

"Watch me pull out first, Beth—make sure I don't hit anything," Clarice said.

Beth backed away.

Clarice turned the key. The motor sputtered and died. The other girls laughed in merriment. So did Clarice. She tried again. The engine caught. With a jolt, the Honda lurched forward, the girls' heads lurching with it, then came to an abrupt stop once more. Now they were all shrieking with laughter, even Beth. Her brothers and sisters had come to the window to watch. Again Clarice got the engine going and had just moved to the edge of the road when Dad's pickup came around the bend and stopped, waiting. Clarice motioned for him to go on; Father mentioned for Clarice to go first. Clarice shook her head. This time Father pointed to the trailer. The girls shrieked again as Clarice put her foot on the gas, the Honda shot out onto the road and chugged off, the girls waving from the windows.

Ray Herndon pulled into their space and got out. "Somebody you know?" he asked.

"Friends," Beth said, unbelievable as it sounded, and went inside.

Harless came over that evening. He was wearing a sweatshirt someone had given him that said BLUEFIELD STATE, and he looked for all the world like the college men Beth saw in commercials on television.

Shirley and Bud swarmed around him again, pulling at his arms, waiting for him to swoop down and tickle them, but he fended them off smiling, eyes on Beth. She got her coat, Harless said good-night, and they left.

It was warm enough that all Beth did was throw the coat around her shoulders as she climbed up onto the seat of the truck. Harless closed the door after her, then came around and got in.

"Ready to see the falls by moonlight?" he asked.

"Only a piece of moon up there," she replied.

"It'll do just as good."

Beth had been down this stretch of road so often—by herself or with her brothers and sisters—that she knew every house before they reached it—the color of the roof, wood or shingles, porch or doorstep. She knew where the trees clumped together and where they were strung apart, knew where the rocky cliff wall gave way to steep, forested hillside, where the trailer court began and where it ended, where the dogs were that you had to look out for and where the ones were that wouldn't hurt you. She could close her eyes almost and tell you when they'd got to old Doc Judy's house, or the house with the FOR SALE: COLORED CANARIES sign in the front yard. She could almost tell you the number of *Register Herald* newspaper boxes they passed along the way.

On the other side of the road, the riverside, she could make out the marsh grass that extended from the bank into the water, knew about when they were opposite the post office over in Crandall, knew every stump where she and Gerry might stop to rest when they hiked beside the river.

But it all seemed different now. More alive, more mysterious. As though none of it had meant anything until this very moment.

She hadn't been kissed since boys chased girls back in fourth grade at recess. Had never been in a truck or car alone with a man except her father in her life. Had never had a man's arm around her except her father's until Harless had touched her the other day. She had a lot to make up for, she was thinking.

Harless reached over as he drove and put one arm around her now. When they got close to the falls, the truck moved slowly as Harless looked for a place to turn in. There were a few spots close enough to the water where you could see the falls from the high seat of a pickup, and in summer they were always taken. Then you had to park in the small gravel lot where the road ended and walk fifty yards or so to the water's edge. Beth knew from the times her father had driven them all there.

But tonight the lovers' spaces were empty, so Harless parked in the weeds on the riverbank. He took his arm from around Beth's shoulder just long enough to turn the ignition off, then gently slipped it around her again as naturally as if it belonged there. Beth shyly leaned sideways until her head was against him, her heart pounding so hard it almost hurt. But it was easy. She was amazed how easy it was to do that. Ahead, through the windshield, the top of the falls was just visible, shimmering in the moonlight. The water made a steady rushing sound that was comfortingly familiar.

Harless turned the radio on low, and Beth was glad that the music had no vocals. It seemed just right.

"Didn't bring a single thing for us to eat or drink," Harless said into her hair, his face nuzzling gently.

"I won't miss it," Beth said.

"Suppose I can last an hour or so." There was a smile in his voice. They sat quietly for a time, Harless's hand caressing her shoulder.

"Dad said you asked once how old I was," Beth mentioned after a time.

"Didn't."

Beth lifted her face, "Yes, you did. Said you couldn't believe I was fifteen."

"Not the same as asking. Never asked, 'cause I already knew."

"Okay, then, you were surprised."

"A little."

"How old did you think I was?"

"Twelve."

She pushed away from him, laughing, and poked him with her elbow. "You never!"

"Eleven . . . twelve . . . somewhere in there."

She laughed again and settled once more against his shoulder. Again the effortlessness of it astonished her. It was as though she'd been waiting for Harless all this time.

"Dad said maybe you thought I was a little old lady."

"No way. Wondered how you'd feel goin' out with me, though, way past your age."

Beth smiled and, without looking at him, asked, "That why you didn't ask me to the party?"

He was silent a moment. "What party?"

"One at the firehouse Halloween night."

"Didn't know you wanted to go!"

"You could've asked and found out."

"How'd you know I went?"

"Everybody saw you. Talked about that orange-haired boy out on the dance floor, girls all over him."

He jiggled her shoulder. "You there? You see me?"

"No, but I heard plenty."

"Was out on the dance floor all of about two minutes. Most of the time I was sitting on the side with my buddies, and if there was girls all over me, I sure didn't know it. Must have passed out from the shock." They both laughed at that. Harless waited a moment, then asked, "You would have gone?"

"If you would've asked."

"Figured your dad wouldn't be too joyful about that—he asks me to drive his babies around on Halloween, and I walk off with his oldest daughter."

Harless bent down then and very gently caught Beth's chin in two fingers, tipping her face upward. Then, as though she were a Christmas tree ornament he was careful not to break, he kissed her lips. A warm, light, soft kiss that only lasted a second or two.

"We've got a date for next Halloween," he told her.

6
_____

So this is love, Beth thought in the days that followed. She was as eager as Harless to be alone with him in the cab of the pickup, nestled together, fingers interlocked, Harless sliding one hand up and down her arm, gently tucking her hair back behind her ear, then caressing her earlobe with his thumb and finger.

She craved to be stroked, kissed, patted—she felt almost thirsty for it—and wondered sometimes how far she would let him go were he to ask, but he never asked. Didn't try.

Was it Harless Prather who would eventually take her away? Harless with whom she'd ride off in a truck—bags and boxes piled in the back—to a new life somewhere? The very thought of it made her tingle. She imagined the entire family at the door, waving good-bye, Douglas and the new baby, too.

"They're all yours now, Gerry," she would say, grinning as wide as a window, and Gerry's "Sweet Jesus" would ring in her ears as they'd head on down Shadbush Road. Next to being in Harless's arms, thinking about him was the nearest thing.

Beth tried to limit her daydreaming to the flower-making sessions for Mrs. Goff, or when she was riding the bus to school. With Harless in the picture, there was even less time than she had before, and it seemed to be schoolwork that Beth was squeezing out. Business math she could handle; in math there were separate numbers, like the keys of a typewriter, all equal in importance, and you simply had to know when to use what. But English, biology, and history were more or less a muddle. When she did well on a quiz, she couldn't say why any more than she knew why she failed one. It all seemed like luck to her—what she happened to study. How did you ever know? Meanwhile there were brothers and sisters to care for, and the holidays coming up faster than she could blink.

The diner was closed for Thanksgiving. Lorna announced that the family would be going to the service at church, and met with howls of protest.

"When you going to cook the turkey, Ma?" Lyle wanted to know, admiring the sixteen-pounder that Ray Herndon had brought home, a gift from the diner. All the employees got one.

"That turkey'll do just fine by itself while we're gone," Mother said. "And you should have your mind more on Him who gives it to us than the bird, anyway."

"George Dean?" Bud asked, naming his father's boss. Beth and Lyle burst out laughing.

"How we all going to fit in the truck?" Geraldine wanted to know. "Last time we went to church we were a year younger and a year smaller."

"I got the truck all cleaned out and some crates back there to sit on," her father told her. "I don't drive too fast and it don't get too cold, you'll get there and back without freezing."

They crawled sleepily out of bed the next morning, and while some took their turns in the shower in one bathroom, two at a time, and others used the second bathroom, Mother washed Douglas and Shirley at the kitchen sink.

Beth couldn't put her finger on it, but they didn't look quite right when they were all dressed up—didn't look natural. Ray Herndon wore a shirt a little too large at the collar and a suit coat with trousers that didn't match. Mother's taffeta dress seemed all wrong somehow, and there were perspiration stains under the arms.

"We look like a bunch of gypsies," Gerry muttered as she sat sullenly down on the arm of the couch to wait for the others.

Lorna glanced quickly over her brood. "Don't see anybody here barefoot, do you?"

"It's just . . ." Gerry looked around helplessly. "Some of us are too dressed up and some of us look like we just came from Goodwill."

"Lord don't care how we look long as we get there," Ray said, opening the front door and herding them outside.

Beth, being the oldest girl in the family, was allowed to sit up front with her parents, Shirley on her lap and Douglas on his mother's, but the others were to sit in the open back. It was Ruth Marie, strangely, who led the revolt.

"Gerry did my hair, Ma, and the wind's going to blow the curl right out," she fussed, refusing to climb up in the truck.

"There'll be enough curl left to see you through church," Lorna said, but Ruth Marie wouldn't budge.

"She gets to sit up front, so do I!" said Betty Jo.

"Sweet Jesus," said Geraldine, balancing precariously on a pair of Mother's high heels, a run in her stockings already.

Ray Herndon came around the truck, unbuckling his belt. "I got to use the strap on every one of you, I will," he said. "Ruth Marie, you get up there 'fore I start with you."

She did then, her eyes welling up, and by the time they reached the church, the truck going not more than twenty miles an hour, the windblown contingent and the five who had been squeeezed together up front all walked through the door of the church together. But Ruth Marie's eyes were red and she kept her head down as they slid into a side pew.

Come, ye thankful people, come,
Raise the song of harvest home. . . .

Beth knew that her father liked to sing—heard him, sometimes, working around the yard, singing softly to himself. But he didn't sing much here. It puzzled her sometimes why he came at all, for he rarely took part in the service. Stiffly holding the hymnbook along with Mother as she sang, he sat and stood when the minister gave the cues, put two dollars in the offering plate when it came around, and bowed his head during prayer. It was as though he belonged to another church.

Beth had a sudden thought. "Pa, you Catholic?" she whispered, just before the second hymn.

Ray Herndon's eyes began to crinkle at the edges and his lips stretched into a small smile. He shook his head, and Beth smiled back. The smile warmed her through half the sermon and would have warmed her even longer except that Douglas was fussing now and it was embarrassing. Even Shirley would just ask a question right out, no thought to where she was. So finally, at a nod from Mother, Beth took Douglas from her and then, her other hand holding Shirley's, led them both out into the foyer where she walked them back and forth along the dark green carpet, stopping at each stained-glass window to let them look.

When the sermon ended at last, followed by the final hymn, the minister gave the benediction and then the organ began its postlude of thanks. The doors to the sanctuary opened, and the minister shook hands with members of the congregation as they left. Beth waited with Shirley and Douglas off to one side.

She watched each person who came out. Why did everyone else look as though he or she belonged here and the Herndons didn't? Was it because the others came every Sunday, most of them, and felt welcome and sure? Was it the casualness with which they dressed, the men with their suit coats unbuttoned, the women without hats? Why did her own family, when Beth saw them there in line, seem so out of place? The look on her mother's face, so eager to please; Lyle's embarrassed smile; the way her father's suit coat was buttoned; the strange hat Mother insisted on wearing to church even though it matched nothing at all and probably belonged to another season. . . .

When they reached the door, the minister shook first Lorna's hand, then Ray's.

"Sure does my heart good to see you folks in church," he said, his smile never wavering. "Be even better if all those children were in our Sunday-school program, nice family like this."

He'd said something similar last year, Beth thought indignantly. And her father's reply was exactly the same, too:

"Lorna and me both work Sundays, Reverend, or we'd be here," he said. "Only time I got off is when the diner's closed."

"Hard to raise children without the Lord," the minister said in answer, reaching down to shake every Herndon hand in line, beginning with Bud's. "Hey, there, sonny, you're getting some new teeth, aren't you?"

As Lorna climbed back in the truck, she mumbled, "He's so intent on the children comin' to Sunday school, why don't he figure a way we can get 'em here?" But by the time they were halfway home, she was humming one of the hymns, her foot bobbing up and down, keeping the beat.

Beth puzzled over it as they moved slowly along in the pickup. The preparation it had taken to get eight children ready, the constant wait for the bathrooms, the clothes to be ironed, shoes to be tied, the open-air ride in the back of the truck . . . What was it that propelled her parents to do this, to endure not only the humiliation of arriving windblown and raw lipped, but the minister's little scolding when it was their turn at the door? Maybe it was their own protest of sorts, Beth decided. "Here we are, like it or not. Count us in." Something like that. To show people that in that broken-down, double-wide trailer over on Shadbush Road, children were being born and properly raised just as in any other family.

"How come we don't have no granddaddies?" Shirley asked suddenly from her perch on Beth's lap.

"Mr. Maxwell can be your granddaddy, Shirley," Mother said. "The Maxwells is coming over to have Thanksgiving dinner with us."

"I mean a real granddaddy," Shirley insisted.

"That thought just hit you out of the blue?" her father said, looking over.

"I saw some in church," Shirley told him. "How come we don't have any?"

"Any man with white hair's a granddaddy to her," Lorna said. "Shirley, both your granddaddies been dead a long time."

"Don't we have no grandmamas, either?"

"My mama died not too long after my daddy. All we got left now is Grandmama Herndon, and she's way off down in Kentucky."

It seemed strange to Beth that it had been Shirley who asked the question that she herself had wondered about for years, but never asked. Had she even thought to ask? She wasn't sure.

"Well, how come we never get to see *her*?" Shirley persisted.

" 'Cause she never invited us and when we invited her she wouldn't come," Ray said, as though to settle the matter. But his answer left a question hanging in the air.

"Why, Dad?" Beth asked.

"Who's to know an old lady's mind?" he said.

Lorna answered for him. "Because, when Ray left Kentucky to come up here and work, his mama didn't like it, that's why. His daddy wanted him to go into the mines along with him, and Ray didn't want to. Wanted somethin' else."

"What'd you want, Dad?"

Beth's father gave a sardonic laugh. "A lot better than what I got, that's for sure." He was quiet a moment. "Heard you could make a living here blowing glass—makin' things. Well, the glass companies wasn't hiring when I come, but the lumberyard was, so that's where I ended up."

Beth tried to reason it out. "But why didn't your mother like it? A person's got to find work."

There was a long silence in the truck, and Beth began to think that neither of her parents would answer. It was like digging down, down, until you struck something hard, something big. You knew it was there but you didn't think you'd ever get it out.

And then her father's voice again: "My mother said once that I was like the engine on a train—I just pulled the others right along after me. Had five brothers and sisters, and they all left Kentucky. Maybe that was just too much to forgive."

Still more silence. But finally Lorna rounded it out: "He not only come up here, but he married a West Virginia girl —me—and that was even worse. Meant he probably wouldn't ever go back and settle there. His folks just closed the door on him. And now Grandma Herndon's mind's almost left her, they say. If we went back now, she wouldn't know him, anyways."

"You ever try explaining it to her, Dad?" Beth asked.

"You ever try talkin' to a mule?" her father said in answer.

And then they were home.

The white-tailed deer season began the day after Thanksgiving, and Beth woke to the sound of rifle shots echoing out across the river, from one side to the other, one hill to the next. It lasted through only two weekends, but Mother didn't like the children outside when hunters were about. Then, abruptly, the season was over and the valley was quiet once again.

Snow came. Beth noticed it on a Saturday night when Harless let her out of the truck. She turned her face up to be kissed and snowflakes settled silently on her eyelashes—large flakes the size of flowers. Beth and Harless stood with their arms around each other, eyes on the sky, letting themselves be frosted, and then Harless laughed and said, "So that's what you'll look like when you're my old woman. White hair, white eyelashes . . ."

"I'm not going to be anybody's 'old woman,' " Beth retorted.

He looked down at her and jiggled her shoulder. "Not going to marry?"

"Not going to let any man call me that," Beth said. He just laughed.

All through the night the snow came down, so that by the time Mother's ride came the next morning to take her to Goffs', and Ray left for the diner, the snow was six inches deep—wet and heavy as pudding. Beth put on her boots and tramped around outside the trailer, testing it out. Wherever she stepped, the snow packed down into ice.

Going back inside and slipping off her boots again, Beth bellowed, "Anybody want to go out in the snow?"

Each Herndon was up like a shot. No one had to be coaxed, not even Gerry, who had begun baby-sitting for a family in the trailer court on Saturday evenings and had gotten in late the night before. Cereal was poured into bowls, the jug of orange juice passed from person to person, faces wiped, clothes changed, and by ten o'clock, Shirley and Douglas were buttoned and pinned into an assortment of jackets and caps and boots, and they all filed out of the trailer and around to the junk pile in back to look for cardboard.

"You can have this one!" Mrs. Maxwell called from the door of the smaller trailer, holding her arm out and dangling a box that a heater had come in. "Saved it just for you." She was a small, lumpy woman in a robe with a sweater over it, her face rimmed with gray hair. She grinned broadly as Lyle tramped over to retrieve the box.

They walked single file along Shadbush Road, shrieking with delight whenever they came to a drift, and each had to try it, thrusting one leg into the snow, looking for the deepest spot. Beth held on to Shirley's hand and Lyle and Bud swung Douglas between them, lifting him over the drifts.

When they came to the place where the wall of rock gave

way to the steep wooded hillside, they began the climb, holding on to roots as they went, hauling the others up behind them, then walking horizontally awhile before going higher still. As they neared an opening in the trees halfway up, they could hear the yelps of boys and girls from the trailer court who had come to slide. The Herndons were welcomed with shouts and information about the sledding path used over the years by area children—a long, narrow path of snow, worn down already by sleds and lined on both sides by trees. It was probably the only incline in the entire woods devoid enough of trees and rocks to accommodate a sled. The path curved sharply near the bottom as it came to an end in a parallel stretch above the road.

It didn't matter here what you had brought—a sled, a plastic runner, cardboard, a metal saucer—the hill was so steep that, having nothing at all but your boots or your backside, you could propel yourself to the bottom. Beth arranged Douglas with Geraldine, Shirley with Ruth Marie, and after the boys had gone down, took the last piece of cardboard for herself and went skidding and whirling almost to the curve at the bottom, rolling off and pulling her cardboard out of the way when she heard a sled coming behind her. She stretched out in the snow on her back in her old pants and jacket, thinking how she'd done this every winter since they'd moved to Shadbush Road.

No one cared that she lay there, enjoying the softness of snow beneath her, staring up at the web of bare branches against the sky—no one thought it strange that she was practically sixteen, the oldest one, and lying in the snow like a puppy. Would Gerry and Lyle take the children out after she had gone? she wondered. And after Gerry and Lyle had left, would Ruth Marie take over? It seemed important that someone do it—that somebody keep up the tradition. When did Mother ever get out and do something fun? Lorna had been an only child; perhaps, without brothers and sisters, she didn't even know how.

They spent the morning on the hill, returning home to make peanut-butter sandwiches and to dry their mittens over the heater, then set off again for another hour. When they came home at last to stay, Mother was already there, complaining about the dishes they'd left in the sink and the tracks on the linoleum.

Lorna always seemed to complain the most in the early months of pregnancy. Later, when her body became swollen and her ankles puffy, and you would think for all the world she'd have every right to moan a little, she seemed to take right to it, walking around at Goffs' with one hand on her abdomen, the other holding a scrub bucket, and would work right up to the last if Mrs. Goff let her, which Mrs. Goff didn't. But now, before her body showed the new life growing inside it, she was irritable and tired and oftentimes too nauseated to cook.

"God *sakes,* turn that TV down," she yelled from the couch where she was trying to nap. "Beth, can't you find nothing else for Shirley and Douglas, me feeling the way I do?"

Lips pressed together, Beth turned off the set and took the two youngest into a back bedroom, only to have Bud come along and turn the TV on again.

By the middle of the afternoon, when Geraldine was washing her hair in the bathroom, Lyle was trying to print the names of his favorite rock groups on his high-top sneakers with a ballpoint pen, Ruth Marie and Betty Jo were cutting out bells and Christmas trees on the dinette table, and Beth had just gotten Douglas down for a late nap, an argument broke out between Bud and Shirley over a sack of pretzels. Lord, but she was sick of babies.

"Beth!" Mother's voice cut through the air like a hatchet. "What in the *world* have I got to do to get me a little quiet?"

Coming out from the boys' bedroom on the other side of the trailer, Beth thought, Well, you could go on back to your own room, for one; quit having so many children, for another, but she didn't say any of it. She walked into the main room to confiscate the pretzels, this time to find her father taking off his jacket.

"I got to stand at the grill all day listening to the counter girls yell orders and come home to arguing, too?" he asked wearily.

"*Told* her to keep those kids quiet!" Mother said, lying back down, one arm over her forehead. "Seems to me I'm going to be scrubbing floors all morning, I could come home to a clean floor myself and some quiet, 'stead of dishes in the sink and footprints on my linoleum and all this fuss."

"Well, seems to *me* you maybe could have noticed how I bundled the kids up and took them sledding and made them lunch and went back up the hill with them a second time," Beth retorted.

"Nobody's saying you don't do your share, Beth," her father put in.

"Well, sure would be nice to have someone notice once in a while." She was pushing it, she knew.

This time her father's words were sharp: "You have to be thanked for feeding 'em and keeping 'em alive? Somebody thank me for going to work every day, puttin' food on the table? Somebody does, I don't hear it."

That should have ended the conversation, and it was surprising even to Beth that she kept on. It was almost as though Harless were in the room with her, standing up for her, making her bold: "What I want to know is why it's *me* you got it in for these days? Why isn't it Gerry being asked to put Douglas down for his nap, or Lyle asked to keep Bud and Shirley quiet?"

"'Cause you're the oldest, girl, and you got to set the example."

"Well, that's something I didn't ask for," Beth said. "Didn't ask to be born at all, did I?" And with that she walked back to her bedroom and shut the door.

It was the first time she had used back talk with her parents—"sass talk," her mother called it. And no sooner had she sat down on the bed than there were footsteps in the hall coming after her. The door swung open and Ray Herndon stepped inside, dark with anger.

"What's that I heard from your lips?"

Beth's heart thumped painfully, and this time her voice was timid: "I said I never asked to be born, is all."

"And you're complainin' that you were? Feeling sorry for yourself 'cause you got brothers and sisters to raise? Want to get yourself a highfalutin job somewhere? Well, let me tell you something, sister. You're lucky you got a roof over your head. Lucky I don't make you quit school the day you turn sixteen, for all the good school does you. Lucky you got a boy like Prather interested in you, for what reason I don't know, 'stead of some punk just passing through." He laid a hand on his belt, but didn't unbuckle it. "You got any more to say about how bad you got it being the oldest, I'll show you how much worse it can be. Come on; let's hear it."

Beth sat with her eyes down, breath coming short. For a full minute, it seemed, her father stood over her, waiting to be provoked. He could yank her to her feet faster than she could think, lay that belt across her legs in a second. So she said nothing, and finally her father turned and left the room.

She stayed motionless on the bed, filled with anger and humiliation. The only thing she and her father agreed on these days was Harless. Without him she was doomed. But as the afternoon light moved across the far wall, Beth was aware of other thoughts, crosscurrents of feeling that swirled around inside her, not entirely new. Like the river, they rose and fell from one day to the next, but they never went away.

Yes, she resented her role as caretaker of the others, but there were some days she actually enjoyed the feel of Douglas on her lap, watching him master coloring, or pounding, or picking up beans with a fork. Yes, she liked Harless, but she *did* want a "highfalutin job," as her father called it. What was so wrong about that? And yes, there were times her school-work, her grades, her flower making for Mrs. Goff, and the press of family seemed overwhelming, and on these days the thought of leaving became incessant—she and Harless driving off somewhere together. But where was somewhere? She didn't know. Would her father be glad to be rid of her? Probably. If not, she didn't care. *See how you get along without me.* Those would be her last words before she shut the door.

But then there was Christmas, and no one—certainly not Beth—would do anything to ruin that. Christmas was what the rest of the year was for. As soon as summer vacation was over, in fact, Lorna Herndon would start talking Christmas, and Beth would begin finding a sack stashed here and there —on a closet shelf, beneath the sink, under a bed—with a child's name on it, a Christmas gift waiting to be given. Mother studied the sales, picked up samples, made things from scraps of cloth, so that when Christmas came, each child had at least one store-bought gift beneath the tree, plus something else made by hand. The rest of the family did the same, squirreling away things made at school, or toys traded with friends, until there was scarcely a place in the house one could poke or pry without coming across a secret destined for Christmas.

At school, however, there wasn't much of Christmas. There was a school assembly in which the choir sang some of the songs from its concert. But other than that, clauses took precedence—clauses and predicates, the backbones of vertebrates, percentage tables, the Korean War, and typing.

Only Miss Talbot allowed some decorations in the classroom, and Beth discovered this when the teacher asked her and Clarice and a boy named Johnny Stone if they would come in over the lunch hour to hang some snowflakes.

"Snowflakes?" Johnny said, pointing incredulously to himself to make sure he was really needed.

Miss Talbot laughed her marvelous, musical laugh. "You'll see," she said. "Get a stepladder from one of the custodians."

To Beth, it was like being one of God's chosen people to be asked. Stephanie King, in all her glory, had not been asked, after all. The silence between her and Beth had grown so ludicrous, so all out of proportion, that Beth wondered sometimes why they both didn't just burst out laughing. All because of Beth's smirky, smuggish grin whenever the typing scores were announced. Stephanie must have thought Beth was laughing at *her*.

She and Clarice hastily ate their sandwiches at lunchtime and then hurried back to the classroom. Johnny was already there, standing awkwardly by a stepladder, glancing at his watch as though planning his escape. But when they saw Miss Talbot backing out of her supply closet, dragging a huge box, even Johnny turned gallant and quickly offered to help.

"There's another box behind it," she said. "They aren't heavy, just huge." And when Johnny had placed both boxes on desktops, Miss Talbot unbuttoned the cuffs of her lavender blouse, rolled up her sleeves, and blew the dust off the boxes.

"You'll never guess where I got these," she said, hauling out three incredibly large snowflakes made of Styrofoam. "Carson Pirie Scott in Chicago." She held one of the snowflakes out before her and turned it around. There were silver sparkles glued to the Styrofoam, and no matter which way the snowflake turned, it caught the light. "I went shopping in Chicago last year after Christmas, and in one of the departments they were taking their decorations down. Every snowflake that was damaged in the slightest was thrown into a trash box. I asked the manager if I could have them, and you should have seen me leaving the store carrying these six snowflakes in a plastic bag."

She set them in a row on the desks. "I've got a faculty meeting in a few minutes, but I wondered if the three of you could hang them for me. Here are the tacks, here's a hammer—they've already got string. You girls stand back and figure where they should go, and Johnny will hang them for us." She looked at Johnny Stone and smiled graciously. "Won't you, Johnny?"

He grinned, too. "Yes, ma'am," he said. He was no longer looking at his watch. He and about every other boy in typing class would not only throw their coats across a puddle if Miss Talbot wanted to cross, Beth was thinking; they would lie down and let her walk on them, she was that wonderful.

"Do you always go shopping in Chicago?" Clarice asked.

"No, I usually go to New York once or twice a year, but I got an impulse to sleep overnight on a train, and the *Cardinal* to Chicago is overnight, you know. I wouldn't have missed it for anything—to lie there in that berth looking out at the mountains against the sky. The lights, that long wail of the whistle . . ."

What amazed Beth was not that Miss Talbot had gone to Chicago or New York. Miss Talbot could fly to Bangkok tomorrow and it would not surprise Beth. Miss Talbot, with her poise and articulation, could say she was addressing the United Nations and that would seem possible, too. What amazed Beth was that Miss Talbot had come back. She couldn't help staring.

There was something else that was different about her teacher—different from other people in Crandall. Wherever Miss Talbot went, she brought something back—something more than snowflakes. Ideas. She had visited a typing class-room north of Chicago once and seen how office managers from local companies were invited to speak to the class. A week after Miss Talbot got back to Crandall, the office man-ager from the State Farm Insurance Company was invited to school to talk. When Miss Talbot went to Washington, D.C., she brought back a new kind of typewriter cleaner she had found in an office supply store there. "If it's good enough for the nation's capital, it's good enough for us," she'd told her students.

Miss Talbot wasn't *afraid* of outside ideas, Beth was think-ing. Mountains could keep you feeling tucked in, all safe and cozy, but they could also keep things out. Good things, some-times. Too often people around Crandall lived their lives a certain way only because that was the way they'd always done it, and their parents before them, which sometimes wasn't reason enough.

Beth and Clarice had fun teasing Johnny Stone after Miss Talbot left that day, instructing him first one way and then another, so that he cried out for mercy as he stretched out his arm, a huge snowflake dangling. But when they were through, the typing classroom had been transformed into a winter palace.

"He's *nice*." Clarice smiled when Johnny took the step-ladder back downstairs. "Wouldn't it be fun if we started dating, Johnny and I? Maybe we could go out with you and Harless sometime. Unless, of course, Harless—being an older man—would find him too juvenile."

"Don't be ridiculous," Beth laughed. But she liked the sound of it: an older man.

Whether it was the transformation of the typing classroom or Beth's part in putting the snowflakes up, her test scores rose even faster. Her fingers pounded the keys in a rhythm no one could match. She was so good at typing her exercises that she rarely even had to look at the keys at all. She kept her eyes on her workbook while her fingers flew from the letter keys to the number keys to the shift key and back again, and for the whole week prior to Christmas vacation, she got the top grade in the daily typing tests. Stephanie King had stopped looking at her altogether. For Stephanie, it seemed, she did not even exist. Beth didn't care. She existed for Harless Prather; of him she was certain.

He was beginning to tell her now where he was on the evenings she didn't see him, beginning to let her into his world, to say when he'd come by again. Sometimes he even talked about how he'd need to start thinking of settling down one of these days. Didn't want to be an old man in his thirties when his children came along.

Often they went to a movie in Crandall, Beth in her new coat, Harless fresh shaven and smelling of soap. Occasionally they saw someone from school, and Beth would take Harless over.

"This is Harless Prather," she would say, and she didn't have to say more because they were holding hands.

And the strange part of it all was that Beth never had to

117

argue with her parents in order to be with Harless. She'd always have Douglas in bed by the time Harless got there, have done her share of the evening chores, and neither Lorna nor Ray asked if she had homework to do. Dad didn't ask if she'd finished any flowers she might have promised Mrs. Goff, either. If it was Harless Prather at the door, Beth was allowed to go. On evenings like this, her father was kind.

Beth and Harless were sitting in the truck at the falls after a movie the Tuesday before Christmas, and Beth's head felt heavy against his shoulder as Harless gently stroked her arm, her side, his hand slipping beneath her coat. Through her shirt, Beth could feel his fingers moving lazily up and down, stopping at the waistband of her jeans, probing an inch or two beneath with a finger, then moving upward again, making little circles beneath her arm. Now the finger was moving closer toward her breast, then moving away, moving closer, moving away. . . .

For the first time, Beth made a small pleasure sound and instantly quieted, thinking of the noises that came from her parents' bedroom. Her face flushed in the darkness of the truck.

Harless's hand paused, then moved in a little closer, and Beth lay her lips against the side of his neck.

He kissed her, then gently took his hand away and put it once more on her shoulder. "Beth, we ought to talk about marrying," he said.

"God Almighty, Harless, I'm only fifteen."

"That's what I mean. I'm twenty-two, and I got a man's body."

She knew then what he meant. Girls always talked about what to do to keep a boy in line, but what if it was the girl doing the wanting? Wanting his arms around her back, wanting his fingers pressing? Sometimes it was as though she could imagine how it was in bed for her parents. She felt the same for Harless. She pulled away from him and straightened up.

But this time his face was serious; the lids didn't slant down at the corners the way they did when he was on the verge of smiling. And when a minute or two had gone by without her thinking of anything to say, Harless slowly withdrew his arm altogether and leaned back in the seat, hands resting on the wheel. "Went with two or three girls I didn't care much about," he said at last, "and only one that I did."

Beth looked over at him. "What happened to the one you did?"

"I don't know." He smiled a little then. "No end to the story yet."

It pleased her. "I'm the only one you ever cared about?"

"Enough to talk about marrying. I don't mean tomorrow. But I'll be twenty-three soon. My dad was married at twenty."

"Harless, there must be a dozen girls around your age wanting to marry. How come you don't want any of them for a wife?"

"You want me to marry one of them?"

"Didn't say that. No, I don't. Just wondered how you come to pick me."

Harless shrugged. "You suppose any two people ever have an answer to that? Maybe I like the way you took care of your brothers and sisters that first night I saw you. Maybe I like your hair. Or maybe it's what your daddy says about you."

She jerked around. "*What's* he say about me?"

"Can't remember anything exactly. Just get the feeling he thinks a lot of his Beth."

"You sure get some weird feelings, Harless. Salvation Army ever come to our door looking for giveaways, I'm the first thing he'd set out by the road."

Harless laughed then and pulled her to him. She turned, so that she lay across his lap in his arms, and he kissed her a movie kiss—long and slow. When he stopped, it was Beth who pulled his head down and started the kiss all over again.

It was Geraldine who upset the family three days before Christmas. She arrived home from school wearing a pair of knee-high boots in fake leopard skin, and before she could get back to her bedroom, Lorna said, "Geraldine!"

Beth was making poinsettias at the card table, and each little yellow bud in its center had to be inserted individually. She turned and saw Gerry pause in the hallway.

"You come here, girl, let me look at you." Mother moved away from the stove and stared at the boots. "Where'd you get those?"

Geraldine sighed in exasperation. "They were a present."

"Who give you a present like that?"

"Jack Carey is who," said Lyle, coming through the door. "Everyone in the whole school saw her trying them on over lunch period."

Geraldine cast daggers at Lyle. Mother sat down heavily on a folding chair, one hand on her back, and put out the other. "Set your foot up here."

Geraldine rolled her eyes and rested a foot on the edge of Mother's chair. Lorna ran one hand over the toe. "That true, Geraldine? You get these from a boy?"

"It was a *Christmas* present, Ma!"

"How much you figure he paid for these?"

"I don't know! They're not real leopard skin."

"What do you think it looks like, a boy giving a girl a pair of leopard-skin boots, her barely fourteen years old?"

"What difference does that make, Ma? It was a *Christmas* present! Birthday-Christmas both! He can give me whatever he wants!"

Shirley and Betty Jo had wandered over to look. Shirley ran one hand over the boot, and Geraldine drew her foot sharply away.

"I don't want no daughter of mine walking around like some cheap street woman over to Charleston," said Lorna. "Give 'em back."

"Ma!" Geraldine gave an agonized yelp, trying to solicit Beth's support, but Beth decided to sit this one out and reached for another petal. "He . . . he really didn't buy them at all. Look, they were his *sister's*! She only wore them once, but they were too narrow and that's why he gave them to me."

"His sister don't even know you, Geraldine!"

"Well, he got 'em from her. You can ask him."

"How old's this Jack Carey?"

"Fifteen."

"How come he's in junior high, then, not high school?"

"How do *I* know, Ma? Maybe he failed or something."

"Well, if he got 'em from his sister, then you got to pay somethin' on them. Only way you can keep those boots, Geraldine Louise, is to give his sister five dollars. Then folks ask where you got 'em, you say you bought 'em from Jack Carey's sister."

Geraldine's shoulders slumped in disbelief.

"You got any money left over from baby-sitting?"

"Not five dollars."

"Well, you give her whatever you got and tell her she'll get the rest later. You hear, now?"

"Yes, ma'am," Geraldine said disgustedly, and went on back to the bedroom.

Lorna went to the other side of the trailer then to change Douglas's pants. When she was out of the room, Lyle passed Beth on the way to the refrigerator and said, "Jack Carey hasn't even got a sister."

"You gonna tell Ma?"

"Not me," said Lyle.

Geraldine was subdued as she and Beth set the table that evening, but as soon as they sat down to eat, Shirley said to her father, "Gerry got new boots with fur spots on them."

"I'm buying them from Jack Carey's sister. They were too small for her," Geraldine said, lifting her fork to her lips and scraping the food off with her teeth.

"Make sure they fit you good, toes don't pinch," was all her father said.

When the meal was over, and Beth and Geraldine were on

kitchen duty, the others watching TV, Beth said, "How come you lied to Ma?"

Geraldine didn't even look up—just went on slinging forks and spoons into the drawer. "She'd make me take 'em back."

"She ever finds out Jack Carey doesn't have a sister, she won't let you out of the house for a month."

"She won't find out unless you tell her."

"Your lie, not mine," said Beth.

The day before Christmas arrived with an icy wind that rattled the metal roof of the trailer and whistled through the cracks. Ruth Marie and Betty Jo, not content with the paper decorations they had already made for the front door, were cutting a newspaper into strips and making a chain to string about the main room. The Herndons' small artificial tree had been set up on an orange crate, decorated, and strung with lights, and when Harless came over about four, Bud and Shirley were already placing some gifts around it. Harless came in long enough to say hello to Beth's parents; then Beth went out to the truck with him.

"Can't stay," he told her as she climbed in beside him. "Mom's got a big dinner for my uncle and his family. But I got something for you."

There was a small box on the seat between them, wrapped in green paper, tied with a gold ribbon. Beth hesitated.

"Go ahead. Not going to bite you," Harless said.

She opened the box and searched beneath a layer of cotton. There was a gold-plated heart on a thin gold chain. She turned it gently about and it caught the light from the house.

Harless switched on the inside light so she could see it

better. On one side of the heart were her initials, engraved, and on the other, the words LOVE, HARLESS.

It was the first time the word had been used between them. Strange, Beth thought, how they could kiss, touch each other's hands, each other's faces, and still be so shy about that word.

"You mean this, Harless?" she asked.

"Wouldn't have had it put there if I didn't," he said. And then, pulling her over to him, "I mean it," and kissed her hard.

"Well, I've got something for you, too." Beth took out a small package she had tucked in her coat pocket that morning, knowing that Harless would come. It was her tenth-grade picture, in a small silver-colored frame she had bought special.

"Nothin' I wanted more," said Harless. He handed her his ballpoint pen, with WHEELERS' BAKERY on it. "Going to sign it for me?"

"What do you want me to write?"

"Whatever comes to mind, but make it pretty."

Carefully Beth removed the photo from under the glass. In one corner she wrote, "Love, Beth," and put it back.

"It's official then," said Harless.

That she loved him? Yes, Beth guessed she did—loved his sweet soap smell, even the prickles on his cheeks where he'd need to shave the next day. They reminded her of the way her father used to rub his stubbled cheek across hers before he shaved—how she'd shriek and laugh and try to get away.

"Harless," she said, her lips touching his face. "I really do love you."

"Beth . . . ," he said. "Hardest thing in this world is not taking you off somewhere and having you."

Her body felt heavy with wanting, and as she watched him drive away, after they'd said their good-nights, she wondered if there was anything in all the world she wanted as much as Harless Prather's body next to hers that very minute.

7

Nothing, it seemed to Beth, could break the spell of Harless's love. It was like a cocoon, wrapping itself all silky around her, insulating her from anything that might go wrong this Christmas Eve. What might go wrong was another outburst from her father. She could forgive his being tired, short of temper, moody, worried. What Beth found hard to forgive was the way he made her feel about herself: as though dreams were beyond her reach—*her* dreams, anyway—and the most she could hope for was a nice boy to love her. On this night, however, that was enough.

The Herndons' trailer was itself a cocoon, nestled in snow in the small half circle just off the road. The Maxwells had been invited for dinner, and they came breathing clouds of warm air, wrapped in old and heavy coats, bringing with them a jar of tomato relish and a batch of popcorn balls held together with red sugar syrup.

They sat in the two soft chairs of the main room, served

by Betty Jo. While Mrs. Maxwell chattered on about Christmases past, her husband grunted in agreement, taking large bites of the baked ham and corn bread from the plate on his lap, looking up occasionally to smile and nod, then returning once more to the business at hand.

Shirley studied them from her place on the sofa. "Where's *your* children at?" she asked.

"Shirley, you hush! Their children's off and grown," Mother answered.

"Two grown men, each got their own families," Mrs. Maxwell added.

"They ever come to see you?" Bud asked.

Mrs. Maxwell wiped at her mouth. "Well, now, Vernon was back three, four years ago to show us his baby girl. . . ."

" . . . and Thomas, he wouldn't set foot in West Virginia again 'less the devil was after him," said her husband. "No sir, he don't like these hills one bit."

"Why not?" asked Beth curiously.

The old man chewed some more, keeping the piece of ham between his few remaining teeth. "Thomas says all the good in West Virginia's locked inside the land; nobody gets anything out of it but the coal and gas companies, and he's sure got that right."

"But . . . it's so pretty here!" Beth protested.

"Can't eat 'pretty,'" Mr. Maxwell told her.

There were times, and this was one of them, when Beth felt she was close to knowing what she wanted to do. If she were asked that very minute, she would say that she wanted to be whoever it was who typed those travel folders that Miss Talbot put on the bulletin board beside the job announcements, award listings, and scholarship applications. Beth never paid attention to awards and scholarships, not with the kind of grades she got in her other classes, but she studied every word on the travel folders. They were always about West Virginia. About white-water rafting near Thurmond, about pottery fairs and bluegrass celebrations, about the Strawberry Festival up in Buckhannon. "Wild and Wonderful West Virginia," the folders read.

There were places you could ski, even, and ski lodges, just like out West. Beth had never known that before, and if *she* didn't know it, there must be a lot of people outside West Virginia who didn't know it, either. Why did folks think they had to go to Colorado to go skiing or white-water rafting, to ride horseback and see bears? If there were enough people coming to see wild and wonderful West Virginia, would there be enough jobs to keep the West Virginians home? Even Beth? She wasn't sure.

Lorna had bought Christmas cupcakes at the True Valu for dessert, with little sugar Santas on them, and the Maxwells watched and laughed as Bud and Shirley ate theirs methodically —first the cake, then the frosting, then the ritual licking of the sugar Santas.

When their neighbors had gone back home, the Herndons debated attending the Christmas Eve service at church. There was no great enthusiasm for going.

"You got to tie me hand and foot before I sit in the back of that truck again," Geraldine said defiantly. "Cold enough at Thanksgiving in the middle of the day. Now it's cold as Alaska out there, you try to ride in an open truck."

"If we go to the Christmas Eve service," Ruth Marie declared, "then everybody who got to ride up front at Thanksgiving's got to sit in the back this time. It's only fair."

"Don't talk dumb," said her father. "You going to put your ma back there?"

"Let's vote," said Lyle.

"I vote no," said Geraldine.

"We could have our own service," Betty Jo suggested.

"Yes! We could have radio music!" cried Ruth Marie. "Can we?"

Lorna looked at her husband. "Guess we can pray just as good at home."

"Way the minister preached at us there after the last service, guess I'm not too eager to feed his collection plate again," said Ray.

Betty Jo and Bud at once set about arranging chairs in rows.

"What's going to be the pulpit?" asked Ruth Marie. "If it's a regular church, we've got to have a pulpit." She pulled the card table across the floor, then set a potato box on top of that, plunking the Bible on the box with a satisfied smile.

Geraldine plopped down on the sofa beside Beth. "Jack Carey walk in now, you never heard of me. Okay?"

Beth, leaning her head against the wall, the gold heart around her neck gleaming against her sweater, smiled contentedly. She couldn't keep her fingers off it. It was like a talisman. Nothing could hurt her this night. "He say he'd be by?" she asked dreamily.

"No, but you never know what Jack's going to do."

"How's he going to get here if he can't drive?"

"He drives," said Geraldine.

"Thought he was only fifteen."

"He is, but he takes his brother's car sometimes."

"You'd be in big trouble, Gerry, if he's caught. Police wouldn't even let him drive the car home—take you both to the station. Dad would skin you alive."

"Jack's careful," Geraldine said simply.

The radio was playing "It Came Upon a Midnight Clear," and Douglas climbed up on the sofa beside Beth, sitting right on the edge, his legs dangling, eyes wide.

"It's just like a church!" breathed Betty Jo, pleased.

"In church there would be candles on Christmas Eve," said Ruth Marie, still not satisfied.

"Little Miss Perfect," said Mother. "I got some birthday candles out there, but they'd be burned down to stubs before we got 'em all lit."

Father began to smile. "I'll take care of the candles," he said, going outside, and a minute later he was back with two flares from the truck. While the younger children gaped and Lyle grinned, Father propped them on cookie sheets, one on either side of the room. They glowed like torches on the Fourth of July.

"Sweet Jesus," Geraldine said, hunkering down in the collar of her sweater and closing her eyes.

"Don't have to have a sermon, do we?" asked Lyle.

"Why don't you kids read us the Bible—each read a few verses?" Mother suggested, sitting next to Bud.

"Then turn the radio down," Geraldine hollered. "Can't

hear a thing with the Mormon Tabernacle Choir singing right in my ear."

When they were settled at last, Mother found the place in the Bible where the Christmas story began, and Ruth Marie took her place at the potato box: "'And it came to pass in those days, that there went out a . . . decree . . . from . . .' I don't know that word, Ma."

"Caesar Augustus," said Lorna.

"'Caesar Augustus, that all the world should be taxed. And this taxing was first made when . . . Cy . . .'" Ruth Marie bit her lip and her face began to cloud. "It's not fair to make me start first; all the big words are at the beginning."

Beth went up, getting Mary and Joseph as far as Bethlehem, then exchanged places again with Ruth Marie.

"'And so it was that while they were there, the days were a . . . accom . . . plished that she should be delivered. And she brought forth her firstborn son and wrapped him in swaddling clothes and laid him in a manger, because . . .'"

"There was no room for them in the inn!" finished Betty Jo, knowing the line by heart, and Ruth Marie glared.

Lyle went next, loping up to the makeshift pulpit. He read three verses with a half grin, then turned it over to Betty Jo, who was already standing, waiting her turn like a racer in a relay:

"'And the angel said unto them, "Fear not: for behold, I bring you good tidings of great joy. . . ."'"

Bud took a turn, reading one verse with help, and then Geraldine finished up with the shepherds returning home and Mary pondering things in her heart.

Mother clapped when it was over, but Betty Jo frowned. "Shhh! You don't *never* clap in church."

"We going to pass the offering plate?" asked Lyle, still grinning.

"Hush up," said Lorna.

"Church is over, then; turn up the radio!" said Lyle, and the room was flooded with carols once again.

It was a festive evening as they finished their wrapping to music. The little service there at home had helped to keep their voices gentle, their words polite.

"I don't think I missed that preacher too much," Father said. "Kids put on a right good performance, Lorna."

"Don't mean we aren't ever going back," she replied. "We've just got to figure some other way to get there than an open truck in December."

"Well, God wants to send me a car, won't get no argument from me," said Ray, and the children laughed.

"A miracle! A miracle!" said Lyle.

"The good Lord send a miracle, He can make it a Cadillac while He's at it," Father added.

Beth felt snug in the warmth of her family that night. Or was it Harless keeping her warm? The thing about love, she decided, was that she never felt alone. No matter where she was or what she was doing, she tried to imagine Harless that very minute. Was he thinking of her? she wondered. And she always figured yes.

"You kids better get off to bed," she told Douglas and Shirley. "Santa come over that mountain in his sleigh and see you still up, he's likely to go right on to Beckley."

They looked at her soberly. Bud, still wanting to believe, however, had questions: "How come he don't go to Beckley first, then come on down here?"

"Yeah, Beth," Lyle teased. "If he's coming down from the North Pole, how come he don't hit Morgantown first, then Grafton, then Richwood and Beckley before us?"

"Well, I don't know what direction he's coming from, but sometime between now and midnight, you're going to hear his sleigh, and you'd better be in bed, eyes shut tight, when you do," Beth said. "Now get your stockings."

Bud and the two younger ones got their stockings and Geraldine helped each fasten one to a doorknob somewhere in the house with a rubber band. When all three were in bed, the rest of the family looked from one to the other, grinning broadly. It had become a family joke—a tradition, Beth thought. When everything was quiet in the two back bedrooms on the other side, they watched as Lyle put on his boots and jacket, carefully removed the collar of little bells from around the cardboard cutout of Rudolph on the front door, and—wrapping them up in a towel—slipped out and around to the back. The others waited, listening.

Finally, far off, it seemed, came the sound of bells. Nothing happened. Betty Jo and Ruth Marie giggled, waiting. The bells sounded again, growing a little louder. On they came, louder still, and all at once there was the thud of feet on the floor in back, and Bud shot out of the bedroom, eyes huge.

"I *hear* 'em!" he said, as everyone else pretended to be busy. "I hear bells, Ma! Listen!"

The others struggled to keep their faces sober.

133

"Bells?" said Lorna.

"There they are again!" Bud yelped, as Douglas appeared sleepily in his diaper and T-shirt in the hallway.

"Santa's coming!" Bud shrieked, racing back down the hallway, and Douglas, shrieking, too, turned and ran after him. Cots squeaked as they dived into bed. The bells jangled once again, then stopped. Nobody got out of bed again, and Shirley slept through it all.

When Lyle came back inside, it was time to fill the stockings. Lorna got out her sack from the dollar store—the hard candies, the whistles and little plastic animals—and Betty Jo and Lyle stuffed the stockings. Beth was just sweeping the crumbs from supper off the linoleum when she saw her mother and father exchange glances.

"We got a little surprise for you all," Ray said, carefully holding back a smile. "Figured it best to open it tonight. Bud and Shirley and Douglas aren't going to be all that excited about it."

Beth set her broom against the wall and waited, wondering, while her father went into his and Lorna's bedroom and returned with a box that he set on the dinette table with a thud. Mother had used newspaper to wrap it in and tied a large green bow on top. "To Beth, Gerry, Lyle, Ruth Marie, Betty Jo, and the others when they're older," she'd written on a piece of tablet paper and shoved it beneath the ribbon.

"What is it?" Ruth Marie cried.

"You think I'm goin' to tell you?" Father grinned. "Open the box, girl."

Lyle and Ruth Marie opened it together while the others

134

stood around. First the ribbon, then the newspaper. *Student Reference Encyclopedia*, it said on the box.

"An encyclopedia!" Ruth Marie stared in awe.

"A whole *set*?" asked Lyle.

"Dad!" said Beth, unbelieving.

Ray Herndon couldn't contain the grin any longer and it took over his whole face. Maybe she had inherited her grin from him, Beth thought. She stepped forward as Lyle removed the cardboard packing and lifted out a book. Then all their hands were reaching, and Beth pulled out a green volume marked *Fen–Geo* and sat down on the couch to look through it.

Lorna could hardly contain herself, either. "Saw 'em on sale at the True Valu, a special Christmas edition, it said, all sixteen volumes for eighty-nine ninety-nine. I come home and says to Ray, 'You think we can afford that?' And he says if God protects his truck, don't let anything go wrong with it the next six months, maybe we can. So I put ten dollars down on a set in November and got 'em paid up just yesterday." She put out one hand and rested it lovingly on top of the box. "Everything you need to know, right in here."

"Wow!" Betty Jo said reverently.

The room was quiet then, with just the sounds of pages turning and little exclamations here and there.

Beth turned the pages in her volume to *Finland—Football—Frog* . . . The article on frogs was a page and a half long with a photograph of a tadpole and another of the adult frog. It told how they changed from tadpoles to frogs, where they lived, what they ate, and how they differed from toads.

The article about frogs in the *World Book Encyclopedia* at the school library, she remembered, was at least four pages long, had a half-dozen photographs, and had three more transparent sheets you could turn over a drawing of a frog, one pointing out all the bones, another the vital organs, and the third the muscles. She searched on through the pages until she came to *Georgia*. Three pages, in big print, and a map. If you had to do a report on Georgia, you could copy every word in this encyclopedia and still not say enough to please a teacher.

This was so like her parents, to buy an encyclopedia from the True Valu. Where would *she* have gone? She didn't know, but for a moment she felt overcome with embarrassment and disappointment. Could not even make her lips say the words that her mother, she knew, was waiting to hear.

"Well, what d'you think?" Lorna said at last.

"Pretty *nice*!" said Lyle.

Still their mother waited.

"They're nice," echoed Geraldine, "but I got to write a report on our state capital, and there isn't any Charleston in here! Got Prince Charles of England, all right, but don't even have our state capital!"

" 'Cause nobody hardly ever heard of our state," Lyle guffawed. "Isn't the encyclopedia's fault."

"Let me see that book!" said Lorna, taking it from Geraldine, and as Beth looked over, she saw the flush of her mother's face, the way her jaw worked when she was upset.

"It's okay," Gerry was saying. "Teacher's got some books at school we can use."

"Never heard of an encyclopedia didn't have the state capitals in it," Mother said, but Beth saw her fingers pause as she came to the place Charleston should have been.

"Well, *no* encyclopedia's got *everything* in it, Ma!" Beth said hastily. "Not even the ones at school. That's why they've got all those different sets. So if you don't find it in one, you can maybe find it in another."

She saw her mother's face relax then, saw the way the tension went out of her father's shoulders. Saw them smile and exclaim over a picture Betty Jo had found of a koala bear. Beth thought of all the weeks her mother had been going to the True Valu, putting down ten or fifteen dollars on the set. The things they'd obviously done without in order to buy them. She got up suddenly and went over to Lorna, bent down, and kissed her cheek.

"Nicest present we ever got," she said, to her mother's pleased smile. Then she went over to kiss her father. Ray Herndon reached up and gave her fingers a quick squeeze.

"'Spect to see those grades improve now," he said to all of them together. But faces were buried in books. Already Lyle was absorbed in fighter planes.

"You all take good care of these books," Lorna cautioned. "Don't want no jelly marks on 'em, Betty Jo. Don't you even take the juice jug near 'em, hear?"

The disappointment and embarrassment had passed over Beth like a breeze. She *was* immune from hurt It was as though knowing that Harless loved her was like a vaccine. Disappointment merely tickled her throat and moved on, didn't take hold. With love, you could take on the world.

Things were even going better between Beth and her father. No wonder love was what folks sang about most on the radio.

As she got up to finish her sweeping, she said, "We got the radio and the TV on at the same time, Ma? I hear somebody talking and somebody singing."

"You got the TV on, Gerry?" Lorna called.

The others looked around.

"It's coming from outside," Lyle said. He got up from his chair and went over to the window. "Ma! Look! A bunch of people out there singing!"

Ray Herndon went over to the window, followed by the others. Cautiously they peered out between the curtains.

"Carolers!" Lorna breathed in amazement.

"Sweet Jesus! Turn out the lights!" cried Geraldine, reaching for the wall switch. "Don't let them see us gawking."

They all stepped back uncertainly, and the lights went out.

"Carolers!" Betty Jo repeated, her face jubilant. "Just like in the books!"

They each found a place in the curtains they could peep out once more.

"Must be collecting for something," said Ray.

"I don't think so. These look like choir people," Lyle told him. They were all whispering as though they might be heard.

Beth tried to make out the figures next to the road. The group appeared to be ten or so people, clad in coats and scarves and caps and boots, singing carols from small booklets they each held in one hand, flashlights in the other.

"Go git the children!" Mother said suddenly. "They got to see this. First time we ever had carolers to our house Christmas Eve."

"We got their stockings filled!" Geraldine protested.

"Go *git* 'em, I said! Might never have a chance to see this again."

Geraldine and Lyle stumbled back to the bedrooms in the dark.

"Maxwells is out on their porch," said Betty Jo. "We supposed to go out there, Dad?"

"We've got to invite them in and give them something hot to drink," said Ruth Marie knowingly. "You always got to ask them in."

Geraldine came back with Shirley, and Lyle with Douglas. Bud followed behind sleepily.

"Santa's come," Bud declared, stopping to stare at the bulges in his stocking.

"Hush up and come look," said Lorna. "Carolers!"

The three youngest children stared out the window in astonishment.

"What have we got to give them, Lorna?" Ray asked.

"Figure I can make something. Bud, put on your boots. All you kids, put on your coats and we'll go out and listen. Somebody drive all the way out here to carol us, least we can do is clap."

Beth tried to see through the darkness but couldn't make out any of the faces. Maybe it was the church choir. She put on her coat, taking Douglas from Lyle and wrapping a jacket around him. She tucked in his bare feet, then followed the others outdoors.

They stood on the steps, Beth in back, holding Douglas. He peered sleepily at the assembly of singers, then rested his head on Beth's shoulder again. A few yards away, the Maxwells were standing together, wearing their coats, smiles wreathing their faces.

"Sure is some kind of beautiful!" Mrs. Maxwell called over, as the carolers finished "We Three Kings."

"You folks know 'Hark, the Herald Angels Sing'?" Lorna called. "That one's my favorite."

"'Hark, the Herald Angels Sing,'" said one of the men to the group, and pages turned, flashlights dipped and rose.

"Wonder how many of 'em drinks coffee," Lorna whispered to Beth. "Got a half pot in there left from breakfast. Could heat that up quick—boil cocoa for the rest."

Beth tried to imagine the carolers coming into the trailer, all trying to squeeze into the main room, looking for chairs to sit down. Were all the dishes wiped and put away? Were there enough cups to go around?

When the song was over, Lorna called out, "That sure is the prettiest music I ever heard. Won't you all come in, have yourselves somethin' hot to drink?"

The man who appeared to be the leader stepped forward again. "No, thank you, ma'am. Just stopped by to wish you a Merry Christmas. And to make sure you do, we'd like you to accept a gift on behalf of the Crandall Presbyterian Youth Fellowship."

Beth was staring at a girl in the second row—could just make out some of the faces now that had turned toward the light from the porch. She was trying to discern the features beneath the wool cap.

The leader walked over to the rear of the van parked nearby and lifted out two baskets. Just as he started in the direction of the trailers, a basket in each hand, Beth recognized the blond hair beneath the cap of the girl in the second row. Stephanie King.

For once their eyes met, and this time Stephanie did not look away. There was a small, sweet smile on her face as the youth fellowship leader handed a food basket to both the Herndons and the Maxwells.

"Merry Christmas!" the man said again. "God bless you."

"Why, this is about the best surprise I ever had!" Mother told him. "Thank you kindly, and Merry Christmas to you all, too. My goodness, you come way out here and . . ."

"Ma, come on inside!" Beth whispered urgently, tugging at her and moving back through the doorway carrying Douglas. Her throat felt so tight she could hardly talk. Lorna looked at her wonderingly, then at Geraldine who had already ducked between them and flung herself inside.

Through the window Beth could see the Maxwells still standing on the steps of their trailer, murmuring little thankyous, Bud and Betty Jo waving and shouting "Merry Christmas!" while the carolers crawled back into their van. Across the way, the Maxwells went inside.

Bud and Betty Jo came back in. "Was that Santa?" Bud asked.

Beth put Douglas on the couch and leaned against the wall, eyes closed, face crimson, as Lorna turned on a light.

"What got into you, Elizabeth Pearl?" she said. "Folks come by acting nice and you to walk off sudden like that?"

"I *knew* one of them!" Beth said, feeling the heat of her own face as she spoke. "One of those girls is in my typing class. She got them to come here, I *know* it."

"Well, glory be, it's *Christmas*, girl! Folks don't go turning down presents at Christmas! What you want me to do, say we don't want it?"

"It's *charity*, Ma, that's what it is," Geraldine declared. "It's like we were starving or something."

"Boy, I coulda told 'em where to take their food basket," grumbled Lyle.

Lorna turned around, staring first at one, then another. "Well, I *never*! In all this world, I never believed I had such ungrateful children."

Betty Jo, however, was already lifting things out of the basket. Another turkey. Canned sweet potatoes. Green beans and cranberry sauce. A store-bought fruitcake.

Lorna looked wordlessly at her husband. But this time Father was on Beth's side.

"Didn't nobody ever accuse me before of not feeding my family," he said, keeping his distance from the basket.

"This makes two turkeys in one year!" Betty Jo said. "What are we going to do with this one, Ma?"

"Git on back to bed!" Lorna yelled suddenly to Bud and Shirley who were inching toward their filled stockings hanging on doorknobs. "Geraldine, put those kids to bed, will you?" She faced the rest of the family incredulously. "What do you mean, what are we going to do with this turkey?"

"We could take it over to some family on Union Street," Beth suggested grimly.

"They don't show any more appreciation than we do, they don't deserve it, neither," said Lorna. "Maybe we ain't so poor, but we ain't so rich, neither."

"Well, I'm with Beth," Father said. "We were all set to

eat ham sandwiches tomorrow, and I don't see nothing that changes it. Anybody want to drive over to Union Street with me, I'm leavin' now."

Mother waved him off. "Well, for heaven's sake, take it, then. You all so high and mighty. Somebody giving me a present never hurt my pride one bit."

"I'll go with you, Dad," said Beth quietly, putting the cans and the turkey back in the basket.

"Me, too," said Lyle, and got his coat.

It was a strange and silent ride into Crandall. This was as close as Beth had felt to her father lately, but it was anger, not love, that had brought them together. Lorna had a heart wide as the Mississippi, Dad used to say. That was the kind of heart you wanted to be around at Christmas, and now all those good feelings they'd had earlier were gone.

"I expect somebody will be glad to see this turkey," Beth said at last.

There was no answer.

Union Street was just behind the depot across the river. It was a short road of small, identical houses, each vying with the others for shabbiness. Though the homes were mere silhouettes against the sky, the street lighting and an occasional porch light illuminated the peeling paint, the broken steps, the hanging screens.

Father slowly drove the length of the street, peering occasionally at a house with a light on. Lyle looked out the other window. Beth, sitting woodenly between them, could not force herself to look at all.

Were they any better than the Presbyterian Youth Fellowship? They didn't know any more about the people in these houses than Stephanie King and her group knew about the Herndons. They were all guilty of making up their minds about people—what they liked and needed—based entirely on externals.

At the end of the street, Ray turned the truck around and started back again, but this time he wasn't looking at the homes, he was looking straight ahead.

"Think there's a mission somewhere over near the firehouse," he said. "Best we take the basket there, I think."

"Yeah, that'd be better," said Lyle, and Beth swallowed with relief.

As the truck reached a STOP sign, then started up again, she stole a look at her father. Were she ever asked, how would she describe him? He was quiet tonight. He was often a quiet man. A proud man. And sometimes angry, too. At her? At the hand life had dealt him? For tonight, anyway, they shared the same feelings. She wanted to inch a little closer to him on the seat. Wanted to lean her head against him, like she had when she was young. Wanted to hear that same fondness in his voice he used when he talked to Shirley. But she didn't move, he didn't speak, and after they'd delivered the basket to the mission, they drove home with only the music on the radio breaking the silence.

8

It was Stephanie King now, not Harless, who was first thing on Beth's mind when she woke in the mornings, last thing on her mind before she slept. Harless's love, she discovered, could not protect her from everything. It could not insulate her from her own hate.

That it was Stephanie King who had suggested taking the basket to the Herndons' was confirmed when Clarice drove out one afternoon, a few days after Christmas, and invited Beth to a movie.

"Got on these old clothes," Beth said, pointing at her jeans.

"Who cares? Nobody will be there in the middle of the afternoon," Clarice told her.

So Beth had grabbed her jacket, climbed into the car with Clarice, and they talked about Johnny Stone—how he'd been calling Clarice every night. But it was when they were sitting in the theater before the show started that Clarice said,

"Thought you might like to know that Stephanie's been blabbing it around what a Good Samaritan she is."

Beth's hand paused over the popcorn. "Like what?" she asked, appearing casual.

For a moment Clarice seemed embarrassed. She stole Beth a quick look, then said, "Oh, saying how her church group delivered baskets on Christmas Eve."

For once Beth's mouth kept up with her brain. For once she managed to stay cool. "*She's* the one who brought that by? We just took it on over to that mission by the firehouse. Figured they could use it." Like it was nothing. Nothing at all.

Clarice laughed then, and Beth laughed with her. The lights dimmed, the movie started, and that was that.

Except it wasn't. For one brief moment, as the credits flashed on the screen, Beth felt a rush of resentment toward Clarice as well—treating her like some pitiful thing without a friend in the world. Then she knew that wasn't true. Clarice was truly trying to be kind, had wanted to prepare Beth for what she might meet up with at school when vacation was over. She needed friends like that.

"You're edgy as a squirrel," Harless told her when he came again. They had gone to the Pizza Hut the last Saturday of Christmas vacation, then driven to the falls.

Beth couldn't bring herself to tell Harless about the basket—about the stupid rivalry between her and Stephanie, and how this, she was sure, was Stephanie's revenge. Even Beth was tired of the chronic bitterness that the anger deposited in her mouth, as though she could taste it on her tongue and teeth. So she concentrated on Harless's arm around her waist and back. On the touch of his fingers. This time, when she curled up in his arms on the seat of the pickup and his hands circled her breasts, she let them stay. She wanted them there, in fact, and let herself go limp as a rag, soberly tracing the outline of his nose and chin with one finger.

There must be something about a girl's face that shows when she lets a boy get personal, Beth thought, because the next evening she was sure that her mother was watching her. Geraldine and Lyle had gone off to the skating rink with friends, Dad was over at the Maxwells' repairing their sink; Betty Jo, Ruth Marie, and Bud were already making valentines in a back bedroom, and the others were in bed. Beth and her mother, in a rare moment, had the big room to themselves.

Beth was at the card table putting together red velvet roses for Mrs. Goff, attaching each petal to a soft rubber base, petal overlapping petal, the most difficult flowers she had done so far, but the prettiest when they were done.

"Got me a few minutes; might as well put my hands to work," Lorna said, reaching for a long green stem and some petals.

"Those go on the outside," Beth told her, pointing out the petals that curled over at the edges, and her mother watched while Beth put one together first.

"Won't be near as fast as you, but I could do me a dozen, maybe," Lorna said. "Mrs. Goff sure picked the right person when she taught you to do her flowers, Beth."

Beth took to the praise like a sponge takes to water, trying hard to hold her smile down. They worked in silence a minute or two, and then Lorna came right out and asked what Beth knew was on her mind: "You liking that Prather boy?"

Beth didn't take her eyes from her work. "Wouldn't be going out with him if I didn't."

"You see him two . . . sometimes three times a week."

Beth glanced at her mother. "You complaining, Ma?"

"No. Wondering is all."

"About what?"

No answer.

"Well, I like him fine. If you didn't want me seeing Harless so much, you maybe should have said something before this."

"Before what?"

Beth could tell from the way her mother's hands paused there on the table that she was hearing it differently from the way Beth had intended. "What I mean is, you've got him feeling like you don't mind if he comes by," she explained.

"We don't mind! Ray says he's a nice boy."

"Hardly a boy, Ma."

"That's a fact." They worked some more, fingers moving warily.

"When I was married," said Lorna at last, "I was just two years older than you. Can't hardly believe it myself."

Beth had never actually thought it out before, but now, when she subtracted her age from her mother's, she realized that was true. "Seventeen? You married Dad when you were seventeen! Then I must have come that very first year."

"It wasn't no shotgun wedding, that's what you're thinking. He just wanted me to be with him—to live with him.

He was lonely, all right; so was I. My daddy had already passed on and Ma was sick—she had to sign for me, you know. Guess she figured I'd be better off married than by myself, should anything happen to her. But a greener bride you never saw."

Beth smiled faintly. "Yeah?" Was she only imagining it, or had her mother blushed?

"You want the truth?" Lorna continued, and now the blush was real. She smiled self-consciously and rubbed one palm against her cheek. "I never seen a naked man till I got married. Didn't have no brothers. Didn't have any sisters, either, to tell me things."

Beth smiled, too. "Guess you were in for a shock." She realized suddenly that she was enjoying herself—sitting here with Mother, just the two of them, talking girl talk.

"Scared to death. We get back from Tennessee, and we only had a few dollars between us, so we had to move in the room where Ray was staying. A closed-in porch is what it was, with a bed in it, not one ounce of heat. Got pregnant right off and didn't even know what was wrong with me. Got to throwing up in the mornings after Ray left for work, and the landlady, she just smiles and nods, won't tell me what I was soon to find out."

"You were seventeen, Ma, and you didn't have any idea?"

"What would *I* know about babies?" It was the way Lorna said it that caught Beth's attention. As though she were boasting, actually.

"You figure that's the way it should be?"

"Well, I turned out, didn't I? Raised me a mess of fine

149

kids, didn't I? Didn't lose a one of you. A woman marries a good man, the Lord'll look after her. Ray never laid a hand on me in anger. You get a good man to head your family, and the rest will follow."

Beth was thinking what the school nurse would say to that if she'd heard. Or Miss Talbot and Miss Wentworth. *Clarice,* even! Wouldn't the girls howl! As far back as sixth grade, Beth knew how babies were made; kids talked. And finally the family-life course in eighth grade filled in the gaps between what she'd heard from others and figured out for herself. Not that she was a walking encyclopedia of sex information, but to be seventeen, as Mother had been, and still so ignorant . . . !

She stole a look at her mother as she worked. "Never wanted to sit down with your ma and ask questions?"

"Huh!" Lorna shook her head. "You hush, now. Why, if I'd ask my ma a question like that, she'd have slapped me clear to China." She stopped working a moment, and Beth wondered if they were both remembering the slap back there in the bedroom. But if Lorna were on the verge of apologizing, she let the opportunity slip by. Instead, she put the finished rose down and reached for another. "Don't you worry, Beth. Time comes for you to know something, I'll tell you. All you got to look out for now is you don't get too cozy with a boy. That's all you got to remember."

Waiting for the bus on Monday, collar turned up against the wind, Beth's heart pounded wildly beneath her coat. Since the school bus passed her house on the way to the trailer court and again after it turned around at the falls, Beth had the option each weekday morning of being out on the road when the bus first came or of waiting for its return before she got on. This morning she had decided to get on early; she fixed a smile on her face as she stepped on board.

"*You're* eager to get to school today!" Mrs. Shayhan said, and Beth's smile never wavered. She looked down the aisle at the rows of seats on either side. There were a lot of empties, just as she had hoped, and Stephanie was sitting in a seat near the back, avoiding Beth's eyes, chatting with a girl across the aisle.

Instead of taking the seat behind Mrs. Shayhan, as she usually did, Beth walked directly down the aisle and slid into the seat in back of Stephanie King.

The girl on that seat turned away from the window and gave Beth a casual glance. "Hi," she said.

"Hi," Beth answered.

The girl turned her attention to the road again as the bus started off, but Beth knew her lines.

"How was Christmas?" she asked the girl.

"Okay," the girl said. "How was yours?"

That was Beth's cue. That was the line she'd been waiting for. "Really nice," she said, "But the *weirdest* thing happened!" She let her voice rise. Didn't care that some of the conversation around her had stopped. Was delighted that Stephanie King had stopped talking also.

"What was that?" the girl beside her asked.

"Well, Christmas Eve," Beth went on, "a group of carolers came by and must have got us mixed up with somebody else, because when we came out to listen, they gave us a food basket. Can you imagine? We didn't want to hurt their feelings so we took it, but after they left, we drove into Crandall and gave it to the mission."

There was no sound at all from Stephanie King.

The girl was still staring. "No kidding? What was in it?"

"Oh, a turkey and a bunch of cheap canned stuff. But it made a nice dinner for someone, I suppose."

"I guess so," the girl said.

Satisfaction rained down on Beth like a waterfall. She could feel the perspiration running down her sides from her armpits, feel it on her back between her shoulder blades. For once, everything had worked out exactly as she'd intended.

She knew who her friends were. Clarice, for example. Since the day Clarice had first driven out and seen where Beth lived, she had never, even for a moment, treated Beth any differently. She had not mentioned the trailer, not made the mistake of giving false compliments. There was nothing to say about the way Beth lived and so she said nothing. It changed nothing. Beth was still the same to her, and it was Beth, not her home, that mattered.

Stephanie said very little the rest of the way to school. When the bus stopped at last, Stephanie hurried toward the front and disappeared inside the school. But Beth, fingering the gold heart that she wore every day now, took her time, and when she went inside at last, she was still smiling.

Two weeks later, the second semester began. Beth had all new courses, new classrooms, and she entered Typing II with great expectations. Miss Talbot was again her teacher, but everything else looked different. Instead of stands to hold their workbooks, there were earphones and dictaphones, with buttons to press and foot pedals below.

Again Beth and Stephanie were in the same class, but they avoided each other completely. Beth didn't know if Stephanie looked at her or not because she never looked at Stephanie now. If Stephanie sat on one side of the room, Beth sat on the other. If they met each other coming down the hall, they each stared straight ahead.

Beth, however, expected to do well. Whatever there was to learn, she would learn it—the knobs, the foot pedal, the new rhythm and order. If her fingers were fast, then her feet shouldn't have much trouble. Her goal, simply put, was to leave Stephanie King behind in the dust. To become the girl from Shadbush Road who was the best typist in Crandall. The state of West Virginia, maybe! *If* she stayed in West Virginia. And so she listened to the instructions carefully, learned each part of the dictaphone, and giggled with the others when they attempted it for the first time.

Agonized groans sounded as feet pressed down too soon, too late. Tapes had to be rewound and played again. Any minute now, Beth thought, she'd get the hang of it, find the rhythm. But as a man's careful voice dictated a letter through her earphones, Beth was dismayed to discover that her fingers seemed unable to follow, as though a connection had been severed somehow between her hands and her brain: *Dear Madam, We are in receipt of your letter of February 9 and regret to inform you that your subscription to the* Cincinnati Examiner *has expired. If you will remit thirty dollars, we will resume delivery. Respectfully yours. . . .*

What was happening to her? Two rows up, she could see

Stephanie King's fingers typing away, no stops, no pauses, hardly. . . . And suddenly Beth knew. It was her spelling. How did you spell *receipt*? How did you spell *subscription*? What about *Cincinnati*—one *n* or two? One *t* or two? How did you spell *resume* or *respectfully*?

She felt the blood draining from her face as Stephanie King took her paper out of her typewriter and laid it, finished, on her desk. All around her, papers were being handed in. Beth swallowed. She was still on the first sentence, still puzzling over the spelling of *receipt*. It was not only speed that counted in the daily test grade, but accuracy.

Numbly, she gathered her books at the end of the session. Clarice had typing at a different time this semester, so Beth couldn't even share her misery with her. And when Beth slid into a chair beside her in the cafeteria, she found that even then she couldn't tell Clarice. It was too embarrassing.

"You know what I heard?" Clarice was saying as she opened her lunch sack and took out a sandwich.

"What?" Beth was ready for any distraction.

"You know that club up near Beckley with live dance music? My sister went last week with some friends, and she said that Miss Talbot and Miss Wentworth were there with their boyfriends and they were both dancing."

Beth tried to imagine Miss Talbot with her arms around a man. Tried to imagine Miss Wentworth dancing. She imagined it very well.

"What were their boyfriends like?" she asked curiously.

"Joan said Miss Talbot's was shorter than she is, with a mustache—really handsome. Miss Wentworth's was huge and bald. Good-looking, but bald."

Beth giggled.

"And she said that *both* teachers danced with *both* men cheek to cheek."

"Miss Wentworth's engaged!"

"Well, she danced with Miss Talbot's boyfriend cheek to cheek, anyway. One last fling, you know."

They laughed out loud, savoring the thought. All through English 204 that afternoon, Beth couldn't keep her eyes off Miss Wentworth, with her gorgeous round face and the prettily shaped eyebrows and the beautifully polished fingernails.

What kept her here in Crandall? Beth wondered. Was it the men? Was it the mountains? Or was it, simply, home?

The volumes of the *Student Reference Encyclopedia* had become picture books in the Herndon household, though Lorna and Ray scarcely noticed. What mattered to them was that their children picked the books up and looked through them often. Mother had cleared a shelf below the window where the encyclopedias were to go, and when someone sat down to watch TV, he or she often chose a book at random to leaf through during commercials. Ray and Lorna were pleased.

Beth looked at them, too, when she wasn't helping out or studying or making flowers for Mrs. Goff. She'd taken to picking up a volume and looking through it for any states beginning with that letter. *I*, for example, netted her *Idaho, Illinois, Indiana,* and *Iowa,* and there were at least two pictures per state of some local scene.

Lordy lord! Beth thought, studying an aerial view of Iowa. It looked like the land had been laid out with a yardstick, all the fields coming together at perfect right angles. Not a hill, not a curve—hardly a tree, even. There were pictures of hills and cliffs and rivers in the volumes containing Montana and New Hampshire and Colorado and Wyoming. But when Beth put the books down and went to stand at her own window, with the sun going down over the hill behind Crandall, she didn't know but what she had a picture postcard of her own to look at every day of her life—changing all the time, too. The sky, the light, the trees, and the water were never the same twice in a row. Some people never seemed to notice where they lived. Folks in Washington, D.C., she'd heard, walked right by the White House every day and didn't even bother to look.

The trailer seemed unusually small in winter. It did every year, but this year was the worst. When the river frosted over, its icy crust crackling alongshore, nobody ventured outside much unless there was new snow to play in. And when all ten members of the family were in the house together, they were bound to get in each other's way.

They were all taller and larger, for one thing. As her brothers and sisters grew older, Beth observed, they filled more space. She could remember a time when there seemed to be more emptiness from the waist up. It was below, around your knees, where you had to look out where you moved, where you stepped. But now, with Geraldine taller than she was, and Lyle fast catching up, there seemed to be arms and hands and legs and feet everywhere. Just having Mother pregnant again made a difference, in fact. When she sat at the card table to eat her supper, she kept her chair pushed out farther than usual, her stomach beginning to show. And more than once, when the younger children went to the refrigerator to pour some milk and came back with a glass, they tripped on one of the legs of Mother's chair. Lorna frequently lost her temper. So did Beth's father. And it was usually Beth he singled out.

"You got to leave these flowers on every chair and table in the house?" he yelled one night when his leg brushed against a box of petals and sent them scattering around the floor.

"I've just about got an order ready for Mrs. Goff," Beth explained, hurriedly picking them up. "Ma's going to take them in tomorrow, and I'm trying to get them packed."

But he seemed not to hear. "When you make a mess, girl, you do it big. Harless ever come by and see what you're really like, he'll think twice. No fella wants a girl who keeps her things like a rat's nest."

Dear Lord Jesus and God, you know how hard it is on this family, and how much worse it's going to get, Beth prayed silently. *Please keep your blessings to yourself and don't send us any more children.* A few more months, and she'd be sixteen, she thought as she stacked the plates at the sink. She could leave if she wanted. No one could stop her.

And then the second thought hit. Where could she go but away with Harless? What choices did she have left? Most of her grades were average at best, and now her one great hope, typing, had been betrayed by her poor spelling. Part of her said, *Harless is the only chance you'll ever get, Beth. Take him and run.* And the other part cautioned, *Hold on.* A civil war inside herself.

That weekend, for the first time, Harless drove her to his

house. He'd taken her bowling, and afterward, as Beth changed back into her shoes, he said simply, "You want to drop by the house, Beth? Mom's been wanting to meet you."

"Been wondering myself what your folks were like," Beth said in answer.

"Just plain ordinary people," Harless told her.

And he was right about that. Beth felt at home as soon as she stepped in the door and Mrs. Prather called, "You two want some applesauce cake? There's some out on the table. Help yourself." Didn't even wait to be introduced. Harless did the introductions, though, then went out to the kitchen, Beth behind him.

She held the saucers while he cut two pieces of cake, and they sat sideways at the dining-room table, facing Harless's parents in the living room. One of Harless's brothers moved in and out, smiling shyly, then went on upstairs.

Mr. Prather was a large man with a round stomach, and he kept the TV going all the while he was talking to them. Most of the time his eyes were on the screen.

"You folks live over on Shadbush Road, Harless tells me," he said in Beth's direction. "Ever get any high water your side?"

"Hardly ever gets above the bank," Beth said, sliding a bite of cake off her fork and into her mouth. She was watching Mrs. Prather darn a thick gray work sock, a block of wood stuck inside it, the long darning needle pushing in and out, dragging a trail of thread behind. Every so often the woman looked up and smiled, and Beth smiled back. She wanted Harless's mother to like her. Strange to think that she might

be sitting near her future mother-in-law this very minute—
that someday they might look back on this night and each
tell the other her first impression.

"Lived there long?" Mr. Prather went on.

"Ever since I was in the second grade."

"What grade you in now?"

"I'm a sophomore."

"Thinking to graduate?"

Beth nodded. "I'd like to be a typist. A really good one.
Get a fine job somewhere."

Harless's mother didn't even look up, went right on darning
the work sock, but she asked, "You work a year, and then
what?"

"Well . . . then I don't know. I'll have to see, I guess."
Beth ate another bite of cake and, because no one else was
talking, felt obliged to keep the conversation going, so she
said, "I just want something to do I can be good at." Brave
words coming from a girl who couldn't spell.

Mrs. Prather's hand moved this way and that along with
the darning needle. "My niece over in Charleston—her ma
paid for her to go through one of those Katharine Gibbs
secretarial schools, you know? Well, a month after she graduated, the girl was married, had her a baby the first year, and
she's got another on the way. All that money going to secretarial school sure would have bought a lot of baby food."

Mr. Prather chuckled genially.

"But she'll still have something to go back on if she ever
needs it," Beth said.

"So what you do is marry a good, healthy man won't get

sick or run off," said Mr. Prather, and laughed again. Mrs. Prather laughed, too. Harless went to the kitchen for another piece of cake.

Beth shifted uncomfortably. "This is very good," she said, motioning toward her saucer. "If you'd give me the recipe sometime, maybe I could make it for Ma."

"Now *that's* putting your hand to useful work," Mrs. Prather said. "Lots of women sit home with nothin' to type, but I never heard of a woman with no cause to cook!"

"Whew!" Beth said when they were in the truck again and she'd closed the door.

Harless just smiled. "They got your number, that's for sure."

"I don't think they liked me, Harless."

"Sure they did." But this time his voice wasn't smiling. He put the key in the ignition but didn't start the motor. Just leaned against the door, away from her. "Didn't know you had all them plans in your head," he said after a moment.

"What plans? Wanting something I can be good at? Figured that should please you, Harless." She noticed the way he kept his eyes straight ahead.

"Just seems to me you got the next few years pretty well sewed up."

"I don't, really. But how about you? What do you figure you'll be doing two years from now?"

"Making a living, that's what. If the bakery don't keep burning the rolls, I suppose I'll still be delivering for Wheelers'."

"You going to do that the rest of your life?"

He turned. "Something wrong with it?"

"Not if that's what you really want to do."

"It's a job," said Harless.

Why did his answer bother her so? Beth wondered. It was a job that paid a salary, just like her father's and mother's, and on that they supported their children, paid the electric bill . . .

"Don't you ever crave to be really good at something?" she asked finally. "I mean, something special you like to do?"

"Never heard anyone complain before about my driving," Harless said.

"I wasn't complaining. Just want to get to know you better, that's all."

He smiled a little then, put one arm around her, and pulled her over. "That's the whole trouble," he said. "I want to know you better, too, and we aren't married."

In the week that followed, Beth seemed to teeter between fear of losing Harless and fear of losing her dream, and sometimes she felt as though she were in danger of both.

For a whole week in Typing II, not only did she not make top grade on the daily typing exercises, she came in tenth or eleventh. Now it was Stephanie King who was smiling, Stephanie King who came off with the top grade, day after day. Handing in her paper on Friday, Beth was horrified to find her eyes filling with tears. She would *not* bawl here in typing class. That would be the final humiliation. She swallowed and fumbled with her notebook a few minutes, head down, so the others could leave before her.

"Beth," said Miss Talbot, when the classroom was empty, "you're having problems, aren't you?"

Beth didn't dare trust herself to answer.

"It's your spelling that's holding you back."

"I know," Beth said hoarsely.

"Here." Miss Talbot came over and handed Beth a small book. "Study this. Really, *really* study it. Take it home and work on it there. I have another copy, and you can return it at the end of the term."

Beth looked at her, then at the book. *Ten-Thousand-Word Business Vocabulary,* it said.

"You're *good,* Beth," the teacher went on. "You've got drive, and there's no reason you can't improve your spelling if you put your mind to it. Every night, twenty words. At *least* twenty words."

Beth stared at her. Why was she doing this? Why had she singled her out? *You're special,* the teacher seemed to be saying, something Beth needed to hear. It was a feeling she used to have about herself but seemed to have lost lately.

"Thanks." She stuck the book in her notebook and managed a smile. "Thanks a lot," she said again as she left the room.

It was not the book that Beth was thanking her for, however. It was what Miss Talbot had said. The words clung to her like plastic wrap. *You're good. . . . You've got drive.* The teacher, it seemed, was the only one who had faith in her lately. But one person was enough.

The first lesson began that night. Beth plopped herself down at bedtime and opened the book. It was a dictionary of sorts, but without the definitions. Just three columns of words to a page in alphabetical order.

"Gerry," she said when her sister came in. "You've got to help me."

"Like what?" Gerry took off the leopard-skin boots she'd worn almost every day. She looked at Beth over her shoulder as she rubbed her feet.

"Every night, you've got to ask me these words, can I spell them, and if I can't, you've got to put a little pencil mark beside them so I'll know which ones to study."

Geraldine reached around for the book and thumbed through it.

"Sweet Jesus!" she cried. "One hundred and fifty pages? I'll be married three times before we get to the end of it."

"We've *got* to!" Beth tried to figure it out in her head. "I've got almost five months left of school. That's twenty weeks, which is . . . uh . . . a hundred and forty days. I've got to do a little more than a page a day, Gerry!"

"Well, I'll be dry mouthed and blind before I get to the end of the first column."

"Please. You've *got* to."

"All I've got to do is die and pay taxes."

"Seems to me a secret's worth something."

"*What* secret?"

"About you and Jack Carey."

Geraldine whirled around. "*What* about me and Jack Carey?"

"About how he hasn't got any sister and what else I can imagine!"

"That's pure blackmail, Beth."

"Gerry, I've got to get through typing. I've got to not only pass, I've got to get the best grade."

"Why? Why do you push yourself like this?"

"Because . . ." Beth stopped. *She* wasn't even sure. "Because I want to like myself. I want something I can be good at, so I'll like myself even if nobody else ever does."

"What makes you think nobody's going to like you? You've got Harless, haven't you?"

"I've just got to be the best I can be, that's all."

Geraldine stood up, pulled off her jeans and her sweater, reached for the T-shirt she wore to bed, and pulled it down over her body. She got under the blanket, propped her pillow up behind her head, took the book, and sighed.

"*Abandon*," she said.

And Beth began.

Throughout the second and third weeks of typing, Stephanie King got the highest grades—day after day after day. Beth didn't even come close.

She said nothing. Neither did Miss Talbot. The teacher had stopped reading the grades aloud and simply posted the results of the daily typing tests on the bulletin board. It was the first thing the class noticed when they came in each day, but Beth even gave up looking at that. She concentrated only on her own work, not the competition.

Every evening she went over the words Gerry had checked the night before, and studied a whole new page as well. She wrote the words she'd missed in her notebook and studied them again on the bus going in to school. There was no more daydreaming on the bus. Twenty solid minutes of study in the morning and twenty in the afternoon meant forty minutes of study a day she would otherwise have been looking out the window. She began to search for ways to conserve her time at home as well. The thought that churned inside her was that if her typing grades went down on her report card, what excuse would she give her father for staying in school unless the other grades went up? And if she didn't stay in school, what escape was there for her? Unless she married Harless.

One of Clarice's jobs in the attendance office in the mornings was to put up new notices about awards and scholarships, and she talked about them from time to time with Beth. But one morning, in a cloud of discouragement, Beth cut her off. "Clarice, you and me are from different worlds entirely. You're looking for ways to get you through West Virginia State and I'm just looking to graduate from high school. Your talking about scholarships and prizes only makes me feel worse. I don't want to hear it."

They were walking slowly out of the cafeteria after lunch and still had ten minutes before the bell. Clarice, her face puzzled, stared at Beth: "I never meant to make you feel bad!"

"I know, but you're on the honor roll! I don't even know how to study. I swear I don't! You've got your books all marked up with yellow, you buy notebooks for every subject. . . . I just scribble things on the backs of test papers. I don't have your smarts, that's all."

"Beth." Clarice grabbed her arm and pulled her over to

the bench by the trophy case. "You think nobody had to sit me down and tell me ways to make it easier?" She fumbled in her shoulder bag and pulled out a thick, yellow marking pen. "Here. A present from me to you. It's a highlighter. You can use it on any book except English, because that belongs to the school, but mark up your own books as much as you like."

"How do I know what to mark?"

"Every time you come to words in italics, highlight them. Anytime you see a list, highlight it. I figure there's at least one important sentence in every paragraph. All you have to do is figure out what it is and highlight it. You'll get the hang of it after a while. Do the same with your notes."

"What notes?"

"You should take notes every time a teacher's talking, because he's the one who makes up the tests. Then, when there's a quiz coming and you study for it, all you have to look at is what you've marked in yellow. Saves *loads* of time."

"Thanks, Clarice." Beth dropped the highlighter in the pocket of her jacket. They sat awkwardly a moment in silence, waiting for the bell, and when it rang, Beth jumped up, relieved. But Clarice still sat on the bench, grinning at her.

"What's so funny?"

"You," Clarice said. "You're not dumb, Beth. You're pretty and funny and clever, and I like you a lot. So there."

Pretty and funny and clever. The words tingled inside Beth's head all afternoon like bells. Well, there were *two* people who believed in her now—Miss Talbot and Clarice, and at least one person who loved her: Harless Prather. Harless and her mother. And Douglas and Shirley. Betty Jo, maybe. The rest she wasn't sure about. Did they love her, like her, or simply tolerate her? Whatever, she could do worse.

It became a game, then—a challenge at least—to look for the important things in her subjects. She delighted in knowing that once she concentrated hard on a chapter and did her highlighting, she would not have to read the whole thing again. She enjoyed seeing an entire section reduced to a few sentences highlighted in yellow. There was something about someone believing in her that seemed to fuel her engine, push her on.

By the second week of February, she began to see a small change in her typing speed. According to Clarice, who kept track, Beth had moved from twelfth place to ninth, back to tenth, then ninth again. She persevered.

The windows of the Herndons' trailer were covered with valentines. Hearts cut out of comic pages, hearts cut out of grocery sacks and colored with crayons, hearts cut out of old Christmas cards . . . all stuck to the glass with flour and water paste.

"Betty Jo, I can't see out the door hardly," Geraldine complained one night. "Car stops out there and I can't even see who's in it, we got so many valentines."

It made no difference. Valentines kept coming. Beth half expected to come home some afternoon and find the entire trailer wrapped in foil. She couldn't imagine what it would be like to have no brothers or sisters. Maybe that's why

Mother liked a large family—to make up for being an only child.

On Valentine's Day, on the way home from school, she was thinking about wrapping Harless's gift. She had put aside some of the money she'd earned from making flowers and had bought him a western-style belt buckle. She also planned to make him some brownies if the kitchen was clear. It being Valentine's Day, however, Betty Jo and Bud and Ruth Marie would all come home from school with shoe boxes full of valentines, and they'd want to sort them on the card table and the dinette in the kitchen.

The bus stopped across the road from the trailer, and Beth noticed a strange car in the clearing in front of it. Somebody visiting Mrs. Maxwell, maybe. One of her sons decide to come back and see her after all?

She crossed the road as Mrs. Shayhan waited, then waved when the bus moved on. She had almost reached the steps when Mrs. Maxwell came out of the other trailer, holding Douglas, Shirley at her side.

Beth put down her books and walked across the frozen ground, wondering.

"What's wrong?" she asked. "Where's Ma?"

Mrs. Maxwell's eyes were worried. "Beth, the midwife's in there with your ma right now."

"What happened? The baby isn't due till May."

"I know, but Lorna's been having pains and bleeding. I told her she should get herself to the hospital, but she wouldn't hear of it. Hour ago, though, I called the number she give me. Midwife come and sent for a doctor. Your pa's on his way."

Beth swung around and dashed up the steps to her own home.

It was strange to enter the trailer and see no one there. To hear noises, but not the sounds of children. They were all coming from her parents' bedroom—pain noises. Grunts. Cries. Like a woman straining, hurting.

The midwife came from the bedroom then, her hands holding a bloody towel. She wasn't the same one who had delivered Douglas. The one who had brought Shirley into the world, maybe.

"You're Beth, aren't you?" the woman said, and then she went into the bathroom and ran some water. "Your mother ought to be in the hospital, but I can't talk her into going. I've got a doctor coming." She lowered her voice and said it straight out. "That baby's dead. I can't get a heartbeat. And Lorna's taking it hard."

For a moment Beth could not find her voice. "But Ma . . . ?" she said finally.

"I expect she'll be all right. The doctor will know."

"Could I see her?"

The midwife nodded.

Numbly, Beth started down the hall and entered her mother's bedroom. Mrs. Herndon lay on the bed with a plastic shower curtain under her hips, a sheet folded up over that, and a towel next to her skin. She was naked from the waist down, sweating as though it were summer. When she saw Beth in the doorway, she made a halfhearted effort to cover herself, then pushed and strained again, and didn't bother.

"Ma . . ." Beth came around to crouch by her mother's pillow. "It help you to hold on to my hand?"

Lorna scrunched up her eyes, grabbed Beth's hand, and squeezed so hard it hurt.

"We're going to lose this one, Beth," she panted, lips quivering like a child's. "First baby I ever lost, Lord help me!"

Beth clasped her mother's hand with both of hers, trying not to look at Lorna's bare legs, at the midwife coming in again with the basin. . . .

She leaned her head against Mother's arm as Lorna strained again. It was not the baby Beth mourned. Her first thought had been that Mother might die and her second was that—if it happened—she would be stuck here forever, raising the others.

Dear Lord Jesus and God, she prayed, *I didn't mean it! Didn't mean for you to take this one back.* But she knew even as she prayed that she couldn't lie to God.

9

It was worse that it happened on Valentine's Day. The hearts on the windows and the little dish of valentine candies that Lorna had put on the table, each imprinted with LOVE YA or HEY, BABE or HOT MAMA, seemed out of place. A love celebration had turned to mourning.

The doctor who came was stern looking—a man in a hurry. When he spoke at all, his voice carried a trace of impatience and disgust. Beth sat on a chair near the short hallway so that she could hear. She was sitting there when her father's pickup screeched to a stop across the road.

"A doctor's with her," Beth said when he came in. "The midwife sent for him."

"She lose the baby?"

"It's not born yet, but the midwife said there wasn't any heartbeat."

"But your ma . . . ?"

171

"She's okay, I guess."

"Best I wait, then."

He sat down on a folding chair across from her, leaning forward, arms on his knees, and faced the bedroom door.

Beth studied his face. How little she knew this man, really. Maybe that wasn't so unusual—girls were probably closer to their mothers, anyway. It wasn't that she just did not know him well, however; she didn't understand the part she knew. Didn't understand his pride in his family one minute and his faultfinding the next, especially of her. Didn't know why it was fine with him that she missed school if necessary to finish an order of flowers for Mrs. Goff, fine when she went out with Harless almost any time she pleased, but not fine to brag about a good grade on her report card, not fine even to talk about finishing school. He would seem, under the circumstances, a man who didn't value education at all, yet the encyclopedias he and Mother had bought—at what sacrifice she couldn't imagine . . . That didn't make one bit of sense whatsoever.

Beth had a sudden longing to go to him, to settle down between his knees as she used to do as a little girl, when he'd rest his big hands on her shoulders, maybe tickle her ear as they watched TV. More than anything else, she wanted a hug right then—a hug of reassurance. Wanted to hear him say that everything would be all right. But Beth wasn't the one on his mind, and she knew it.

Ray Herndon nervously pushed the palms of his hands together, then bent his fingers and cracked the knuckles of first one hand, then the other.

"Lorna fall or bump herself?" he asked finally.

"The midwife didn't say, Dad. Just said she tried to get Ma to go to the hospital, but she wouldn't."

"No, didn't think she would. Her own ma went into the hospital when she was sick and never come out again. Lorna figured her mother would've got better if she'd stayed home."

"You can't always judge one thing by another," Beth told him, then realized that this wasn't conforting. "If the baby didn't have any heartbeat, though, it could have been dead before she even got to the hospital. Maybe it wouldn't have helped."

"That's pretty much what I figured."

It was another hour before the doctor came out of the bedroom, holding his black bag in one hand, his suit coat thrown over his arm.

"Mr. Herndon?" he said.

Ray stood up quickly, as though snapping to attention. The doctor gave his hand a brief shake.

"I'm sorry, but as you've guessed, I suppose, she lost the baby," the doctor said. He observed a moment of professional silence, eyes down. "But your wife is as well as can be expected. I would prefer that she be in the hospital, of course, where we could keep an eye on her for a day or so, but—since she won't go—I've done what I can. I don't think there will be any problems. I left some prescriptions with the midwife, and she'll check on her again tomorrow."

He put his bag down and slipped on his suit coat. "As for future babies, your wife has some cervical tearing from past births, and this makes it more difficult to hold the fetus. If she has more pregnancies—if you insist on having more children—and you already have eight, I understand . . . ?" He waited for Father's nod, then went on, "Then she should have some repairs done, or this will happen again."

"She'd have to go into the hospital for that, Doctor?"

"Of course!" This time the doctor did not try to disguise his irritation. "I'm not a veterinarian, Mr. Herndon. I don't go around doing surgery just anywhere."

Beth felt a rush of anger and embarrassment. Her father's face reddened, but he didn't move. Didn't even blink. The doctor recovered somewhat and added, "She would need the best of care, is what I'm saying, and a sterile hospital environment is what she should have. You understand."

Ray nodded again, the doctor nodded in turn to Beth, opened the door, and left. When Beth turned again toward her father, he was already going down the hall to the bedroom. The midwife closed the door after him.

Beth walked slowly to the window. The rest of the children had come home from school, and Mrs. Maxwell had managed to snag them before they came into the trailer. They stood outside now like the crowd scene in a movie, watching the doctor leave. Each of them, herself included, had come into this world taking a little bit from Mother, Beth thought. Whether what they'd brought her was more than what they'd taken, only a mother could figure, and maybe she couldn't do that until the children were grown.

The doctor's car was starting up and moving on out into the road. The minute he was gone, the Herndon children slunk toward the house, first Lyle, then Geraldine, then Ruth

Marie and Betty Jo, and finally all but the two youngest had come in and were sitting silently around the main room, still in their coats.

"Ma had the baby early and it died," Beth told them, "but she's doing okay, and you're all going to have to help a little more until she's strong again. Keep her off her feet for a few days."

No one said anything.

"Gerry," Beth went on, "I'm going to help the midwife clean up that bedroom. You've got to get supper tonight."

"You don't have to tell me; I figured that already," Gerry snapped.

Beth sighed. She wasn't the only one to whom another baby, born or lost, meant more work, less time for the rest of them. But there would be no more babies now, the doctor had said—live babies, anyway—unless Mother had an operation, which she would surely not do. The Lord, if it *was* the Lord, had answered Beth's prayer once and for all.

There was no sound at all in the house except the scraping of Gerry's knife in the kitchen as she peeled the potatoes for dinner, clunking the knife in the sink when she was through, then banging the pan on the stove.

Beth went from ninth place in typing class down to seventh, then sixth, and back to seventh again. Gerry's help with her spelling lists had lasted all of two weeks. Now, when Gerry came to bed, she claimed she was too tired to read.

Beth tried to enlist Lyle to help, but he had trouble pronouncing the words. Mother, of course, was not to be bothered, and when Beth asked her father one evening if he would mind reading off one or two columns to her, he said he had better things to do: "You want to study a dictionary, you study by yourself."

"I can't, Dad! Can't tell if I know how to spell the words or not if I'm looking right at them!" Anger rushed up her throat and danced on her tongue. "I'd think you'd be *pleased* I want to get ahead in school. And maybe you do have better things to do, but it doesn't seem to me that TV's one of them." She could hardly believe what she'd said.

Ray Herndon jerked about as though her reply had caught him by the hair.

"You aching for a slap, girl? You think I work all day on my feet at the grill and don't have the right to rest myself and watch a little TV?"

Her words rushed on. "I *know* you're tired. I *know* you've got that right. But I'm trying my best to do good at something, and it doesn't seem like I get any help around here whatsoever."

"You got friends, don't you? Got sisters, don't you?"

She dropped it then. Maybe there were problems she didn't know about—money problems, health problems. . . . She solved it finally by offering Ruth Marie a dime every evening for reading a page of words. Ruth Marie proved good enough to sound them out if she didn't know them on sight, and Beth moved from seventh to fifth place in typing. Stephanie King had firm hold on first.

"I think she's looking to get herself a scholarship out of state, Radcliffe or something," Clarice told Beth one afternoon in gym.

"She'll make it," Beth said dully, eating only half her sandwich and putting the rest away. "She's got brains, talent, looks, money. . . ."

"So?" said Clarice. "You've got brains, too, Beth Herndon. You've also got Harless Prather."

It didn't sound equal, somehow. Beth said nothing.

"There are other girls who'd like to go out with him," Clarice went on. "Maybe you're luckier than you think."

"Maybe," Beth said.

Mother had begun working at Goffs' again, but Beth usually found her lying on the couch when she got home from school. The household, for the most part, was back to normal except for the sadness that Lorna dragged around with her. Beth sat on the sofa beside her one day in early March when she got in—when Shirley and Douglas were playing beneath a blanket they'd thrown over the card table—and tried to think of what she could say that would be helpful. Everything she ran through her head seemed wrong.

"Shadbushes are blooming, Ma," she ventured. "Saw some of those white flowers up on the ridge when the bus made the turn."

Lorna smiled a little. "Serviceberry, that's what we used to call them bushes," she said. "Ma told me why, but I bet you can't guess."

"No, I can't." Beth smiled back.

"Well, seems like the circuit preachers couldn't get into the backwoods places to preach during the winter, and when the white flowers of the shadbush bloomed in early spring, the folks would know that church services were starting up again. That's why."

"I never heard that," said Beth. "Might be I could climb up and get some for you."

"That'd be nice, but flowers in the house right now would seem too much like a funeral."

For a time Beth was quiet. "Well, Ma, at least it wasn't your first baby," she said at last. "You've got eight other children to keep you busy."

"That's true enough, but it's always the one you lose you think on," Lorna said, and sighed. "That's what Mrs. Maxwell told me, anyway; she lost one when she was younger."

Beth sat silently flipping through the pages of one of the encyclopedias. She was looking up *Pregnancy*, actually, to see if it contained anything helpful. There was no entry at all for *Pregnancy*. Beth reached for the *San–Spa* volume and looked up *Sex*. "Sex," it read. "See Reproduction." She gave up trying to find anything that would help Mother, but wondered if there might be something here to help the younger children when they had questions. She put the *San–Spa* book back and reached for the one with the *R*s.

"The thing is," Mother was saying, "I knew something was wrong the night before it happened. Pains started just after I'd gone to bed. I was hoping if I kept myself still, didn't move, I could stop it, maybe; didn't even tell Ray. But when the bleeding began, I knew that baby was lost. Kept thinking, though, could I have saved it if I'd gone to the hospital?" She turned her face toward the back of the sofa, and Beth watched a tear run a zigzag course down her cheek.

"Probably couldn't have, Ma. It'd be three months early! You can't go thinking 'what if,' " Beth said, but now her mother was crying silently.

Beth sat waiting for the tears to stop, and when they did, her mother said, "Only thing I've got to leave behind me when I die is my children."

"Oh, Ma . . ." Beth gently patted her hand.

"It's true." Lorna sniffled and propped a pillow up behind her back. "All I got to show I was here, you know? *Lorna Herndon passed this way.* Only thing to show I was alive: I left children. Makes 'em all precious, even the one I lost."

The room was still except for Douglas and Shirley's chatter beneath the card-table house.

Beth eyed her mother and a trace of a smile played about her lips. "We could put it on a T-shirt," she offered at last.

Lorna turned her head. "What?"

Beth's smile grew wider. "We could all eight of us go around in T-shirts with the words ONE OF LORNA'S KIDS on them."

Mother smiled at last. Laughed, even. Then she closed her eyes again and settled down for a short nap before the others got home, and Beth moved over to a chair with the encyclopedia.

She found the *R*s and looked up *Reproduction* to see what Betty Jo would learn if she ever looked. The article was divided into two sections, *Asexual Reproduction* and *Sexual Reproduction*, and under the second section was a heading titled "Fertilization and Development." Her eyes traveled down the page, from flowers to frogs to salamanders. And finally, one short paragraph that would be of any use to Betty Jo at all: "In most animals," it said, "fertilization is internal. The male inserts the sperm directly into the female's body where the sperm unites with the egg to form the embryo."

This was it? This was the most Betty Jo and Ruth Marie and Shirley would learn about sex from this entire set of books? She tried to imagine what Shirley would picture if anybody read that paragraph to her. *Where* in the female? And *how* did the male do it? What kind of book was this that told so little when there was so very much to tell? Beth put the book back and went to the stove to start supper.

March moved on methodically, one blustery day following another. The moon-white bark of the sycamores matched the cold white of the sky as clouds raced across it in one final winter fling. The murmur of the river had become a roar as the water level reached its peak, and the rocks that sunned themselves in autumn were no longer visible beneath the froth of the churning current.

What also became a roar was something inside Beth herself, her determination that Mother's lot would not be her own, or that, if a new baby *did* manage to hold on and get itself born, it would not be Beth who had to spend the rest of her life caring for it.

In the first grading period of the new semester, Beth's grade in typing fell, but her other grades rose a little, thanks to the study tips Clarice had given her, plus a few that Beth discovered for herself. When there was something difficult to memorize, for example, she didn't wait until the night before the test to cram it in, but ran through it once or twice a day a week beforehand, letting it get a good foothold in her head.

In history, old Mrs. Stoddard—her breath as sour as her expression, her voice as musty as her texts—droned on about

Third World countries and the balance of trade, but Beth forced her mind to pay attention, demanded that her fingers take notes during class. Biology, never a favorite, at least came easier because she could visualize a vertebrate, whereas the balance of trade brought no picture to mind at all.

Beth talked about her grades to no one, not even Clarice. She put her report card on the table with the others when she got home, but did not mention it. She was working now for something more than grades.

She moved back and forth between sixth and fifth place in the daily typing exercises, and it was a small advance like this, plus her daily spelling sessions with Ruth Marie, that gave her any feeling of progress at all.

"Likelihood," said Ruth Marie.

"L-i-k-e-l-e-h-o-o-d," spelled Beth.

"Wrong!" Ruth Marie sang out, making a pencil check. She always announced the errors with gusto, which Beth ignored.

"Limitation."

"L-i-m-i-t-a-t-i-o-n."

"Lim . . . I guess it's *limousine,"* said Ruth Marie.

"Check it," said Beth. "I haven't the foggiest idea."

The valentines on the windows of the trailer had been replaced with green shamrocks, and when April came, ushered in by mists and a pale, feathery green on the hill behind Crandall, the shamrocks gave way to rabbit cutouts, colored eggs, and drawings of yellow chicks on grocery-sack paper. Betty Jo and Ruth Marie used crayons until they were worn down to little stubs, and with the money she had collected so far from Beth for the spelling lessons, Ruth Marie invested in a sixty-four-color Crayola set, including copper, burgundy, and gold.

Beth realized that holidays were, for the family, a break in monotony, a link with the rest of the community, which put up decorations in the library and stores. Holidays meant that there was something to anticipate just around the corner and that when it came, things might be better somehow. She asked Harless once what he looked forward to, and he said right off, without half thinking, the day his truck was paid up.

She was living a double life, Beth began to feel. There were times at school when she was studying hard that she didn't think of Harless at all, when she would raise her head from a book, slowly coming back into the present, and realize suddenly, strangely, that she had a boyfriend. Yet when she was with him, circled by his arms, the rest of the world didn't matter—just Beth and Harless, on and on.

She did not talk about school much to him. Didn't even tell him about the spelling dictionary and how much better she'd done since January. She seemed to understand that talk like this was a wall between them and, in their time together, ignored the wall.

Each evening they spent in his truck, they went a little further "being cozy," as Mother would put it, than they had before. If Betty Jo and Ruth Marie lived from one holiday to the next, Beth lived for the surprise of Harless's hands or kiss, and the way his lips brushed her skin. She touched him, too—let her hands explore the back of his neck, dip down into the collar of his shirt, as the breeze wafted in through the open windows of the pickup. No longer did Harless have to keep the heater on or bring a blanket to put over them as they snuggled together on the seat. Spring urged them on, made it soft and sweet. Made it easy.

At the end of the first week in April, as Beth was preparing for an evening with Harless, when a light wind came through the bathroom window, fluttering the shower curtain, bringing with it the fragrant whiff of new grass and some sweet flower about to bloom, she felt soft herself—spongy—like new earth.

She put on a thin gauze blouse, tucking it down into her jeans, and a denim jacket over that. She had used a new shampoo on her hair that made it shine, and as she took one last look in the bathroom mirror, she whispered "Beautiful Beth" to her reflection, then laughed at her foolishness.

She walked down the short hallway to the main room of the trailer, her soft-soled shoes making no sound on the floor, and was surprised to see her father sitting on the sofa looking through her business dictionary. As she crossed over to the window to see if Harless had come, she said, "I'm up to *M* now, Dad. That's halfway through the alphabet—more than halfway, if you leave out the *X*s."

He put the book on the cushion beside him and reached forward to change channels on the TV. And when he didn't reply, Beth added impetuously, "Once I know all those words in that book, I'll bet I could get me a job anywhere I want." She whirled around in the center of the floor, propelled by her own exuberance. "Chicago, even! New York City!" It was hot air and she knew it, but she was feeling good. Spring had settled in her bones.

"Well, a girl look like you look, I guess she's got to take

all the help she can get," Ray Herndon said in reply, something of a smile in his voice.

"*How* do I look?" Beth asked, glancing quickly down at her feet and legs.

"You want the truth, girl?"

"Sure I do."

"Too short, too skinny, waist's too thick, lips too thin, nose too pinched, and your eyes are faded. Now that's a true picture postcard." He laughed.

She stared at him, waiting for the admission that, on the contrary, she'd never looked better.

"I thought I looked pretty nice," she said at last.

"Well, honey, you sure ain't no beauty, and why Harless takes to you, I can't imagine, but maybe you're just lucky."

Beth heard the tires of Harless's truck on the ground outside, saw the sweep of headlights on the wall. But still she waited. A second more and her father would tell her to go on, she looked great, but when he glanced up again, he looked surprised to see she was still there and shot her a quizzical look. Beth's eyes welled up. She lunged for the door, flung herself down the steps, and groped blindly toward the truck.

Inside, on the seat, she cried.

"What is it, Beth? What's the matter?"

"Oh, Harless, I think I hate him."

"Who?"

"Dad."

He put an arm around her, pulled her over, and Beth cried some more. Just let the tears come.

"What'd he say? You know how he likes to tease."

"He wasn't teasing." Beth took a tissue out of her pocket, blew her nose, then laid her head again on Harless's shoulder. Slowly, sniffling, she told him word for word what had been said.

"You know what he makes me feel like, Harless? Dumb and ugly, like the only lucky thing about me is I'm alive and I've got you."

He stroked her arm. "Well, I can't figure him either, Beth. Maybe he's got a pain somewhere making him mean." He sat silently for a full minute, holding her, before he said finally, softly, "You still want to see that movie with me?"

"Yes," Beth said. "Let's go. I'm over it now."

But she wasn't. They went to the theater and watched a detective thriller, and Beth hardly watched. She felt bruised, black and blue, not on her body but on her spirit. Worse than the words her father had spoken was her certainty that he had deliberately wanted to hurt her, to humiliate her, to send her out to Harless feeling cowed and stupid. The why of it was beyond all comprehension.

She felt so vulnerable that it seemed to her miraculous she was here with Harless at all, that it was his arm that was around her now, his fingers that were interlocked with hers, his thumb running over the thin web of skin between her fingers, making her shiver. That he could love her—*like* her, even.

Something strange was happening between them that night. Beth felt it and she knew that Harless did, too. Ordinarily, in a show like this, Harless got caught up in the film and scarcely noticed her again until it was over. Tonight, however, it seemed as though both of them were just waiting for the show to end. They went to the drive-in afterward, ordered shakes, and the moment they had finished, Harless blinked his lights, the red-capped girl took the tray, and Harless started the engine.

He drove past the falls this time and on beyond the parking lot to where the road ended, giving way to underbrush, trees, and rocks. He found a place and turned the engine off.

Everything moved in slow motion: Harless's hands unbuttoning her blouse, Harless's palms on her bare shoulders. Everything he touched was followed by a kiss. Beth, too, touched Harless in places she had not touched before, urged on by his quick intake of air when her fingers surprised him. She lay in his arms, both of them bare to the waist, and Harless stroked her breasts.

"You're so beautiful, Beth," he said. "What your dad thinks of you and what comes out of his mouth are two different things entirely. You've got to remember that."

She loved his words, true or not.

"Know what your dad first said to me when I told him I was twenty-two? Said I should think about marrying. And when I told him I'd been giving it some thought but hadn't found the right girl yet, he said I should meet his Beth. 'Pretty,' he said, and 'quick as a cracker.'"

"He said that?" Beth opened her eyes.

"Those were his very words—'pretty.' Said you had real pretty hair."

"And he said you should *marry* me?"

Harless smiled. "Didn't come right out and say so. Said I

should *meet* you. Guess he figured the rest was up to us. You *are* beautiful, Beth, and he knows it."

She loved his voice, loved his touch, loved the misty darkness and the smell of spring around them, the sound of the falls. She also knew that the more intimate they were with each other, the closer they would want to be and the harder it would be to wait.

For tonight, perhaps, they would be content to press against each other, skin to skin, his chest and her breasts bare, but next time they'd want more and the time after that, and Beth craved him every bit as much as he wanted her.

"It's not fair to you, Harless," she said finally.

"Only fair thing to either of us is to get married. You name the month. The year, even. You want to finish school first, we can marry the day after you graduate; your folks would sign. But if you want to marry first when you're sixteen, you could still finish high school, if that's what you got your heart set on. I won't be against it."

She pressed her lips against his shoulder and thought about starting her junior year as Mrs. Harless Prather. Tried to imagine Stephanie's face if she came back to school with a ring. Clarice's, even. Is that what she wanted?

There were a few other girls in school, most of them seniors, who had engagement rings already—one who'd left school last year to marry and never came back. This was *crazy*, she thought suddenly, startled. She was a month shy of being sixteen, and she would still be the youngest married girl in school. The *only* married girl in Crandall High, for all she knew.

"Harless," she said, catching his hand and holding it so that he couldn't distract her. "There's nobody else in high school who's married."

"Aren't afraid to be the first, are you?"

Why, she wondered, was it always the Herndons standing out? The Herndons with eight kids in the family and, until recently, another on the way? The Herndons in a house trailer off the side of the road, not even in a regular trailer court? The Herndons riding to church on Thanksgiving in the back of a pickup? And now, possibly, one of the Herndons, naturally, the first in high school to marry. . . .

She let him hold her again and hugged his shoulders tightly as if to keep from thinking what was already going through her head, to keep from saying the words that were lining up in her mouth. Holding on to him as though, if she didn't, he might get away, or *she* might go.

If she married when she was sixteen, she'd be even a year younger than her mother was when *she* was married. She'd be repeating the pattern once again—the early marriage, the babies, probably. . . . It was as though her parents *wanted* this. All these evenings when she could have been helping out around the house, they'd let her go. Encouraged her.

She sat up, suddenly shivering.

"You cold?" Harless asked.

She nodded.

"Put my shirt around you."

She did, hugging herself with her arms, and Harless rolled up one of the windows.

"How would we ever manage it, Harless, you and me married, me in school, and you with your truck to pay for?"

"Always live at my house for a while. We got room."

She drew in her breath and held it. "I don't know," she said at last. The image of her parents came to mind, sleeping on a closed-in back porch, her mother pregnant, the landlady smiling slyly. . . . "We'd be starting off without anything to call our own, just sharing a bed in your parents' house."

"Beats driving out here to the falls," he told her.

He was right about that.

"Your dad would probably help out some," Harless ventured.

"I doubt it."

"Told me he would."

She jerked about. "Told you he'd what?"

"Said that if we were to marry, he knew it would be hard for us for a while, and he'd help out with the truck payments."

"With your truck payments?" Her chest suddenly felt icy cold. "Harless, he can't hardly meet his own truck payments. What makes him think he can take on yours?" Her teeth began to chatter, and Beth suddenly reached for her clothes and began putting them on.

"Beth?" Harless put one hand on her arm. "Listen, you upset? I wouldn't take money from your dad if he couldn't afford it. Maybe he was just talking big, I don't know. I was just telling you what he said, is all." And when she didn't answer, went on buttoning, Harless said, "Beth, what'd I say?"

"What you said, Harless, was that my dad's paying you to take me off his hands."

"I never said that!"

"Well, that's the sense my ears made of it." She felt the sting of tears in her eyes already and fought against them.

This time, her anger helped hold them back, but she had never felt so unwanted, so useless, so ugly, so dumb. . . . It seemed the final irony.

"Beth!" Harless reached over and took both her wrists. She could see his face in the moonlight and she knew she'd hurt him. "It wasn't like that at all. You dad's not selling and I'm not buying. If I didn't love you, we wouldn't even be here talking this way."

She believed him, but she didn't feel pretty any longer. She felt more like a sixteen-year-old Lorna, ignorant of life, of men, of what lay ahead. Why were her parents so eager to have her repeat their life? Why was she so hungry to go along? She did love Harless, she knew she did. And yet . . .

Dressed, she sat on her side of the seat, staring at the river through the windshield—at the blackness of the night and the occasional gleam of light on the surface of the water. Finally Harless put on his shirt, and still they sat, each far over on his own side of the seat.

"Can't figure you out," Harless said finally. "One minute I got you against my chest, and the next you're all prickly, can't get near you."

"I'm sorry," she said, but even when he put one hand on her knee, she made no move to get closer.

Harless withdrew his hand. "Seems to me you turn on me this way, I got an explanation coming."

What was there to explain? That her father didn't love her? Did she have to sit here and painfully point that out? Did Harless really expect her to spell out in black and white just how lucky she was that he was willing to marry her—no looks, no skills, no money?

"I'm just feeling all mixed up in my head," she said at last. "I don't hardly know myself."

Harless waited a while longer, but when Beth said nothing more, he finally turned the key in the ignition and backed out onto the road.

When they reached her home, he didn't turn off the engine, just sat idling the motor. "Beth," he said, "you want to see me again?" His voice was gentle, but far too polite. She cringed at the coldness in it.

"I still love you, Harless," she said in reply.

"Nice to hear, but it doesn't answer the question."

"Yes, but maybe not right away. I've got to think this out."

"How long you figure it will take to do that?"

"I don't know."

It was after eleven, she remembered from the clock on his dash, and the trailer was dark. Only the bare bulb burned on the porch. Beth stood in the shadows and watched Harless's pickup move out into the road again, watched until the two red taillights disappeared around the bend, listened as the sound of the engine grew fainter and fainter until finally there was no noise at all but the rush of the river.

For some minutes Beth stood rooted to the ground, unable to move, to blink, even. And suddenly she turned away from the trailer and began walking back up Shadbush Road in the direction of the falls. She walked until she came to the little overhang in the rocks and then, climbing up ledge after ledge, hoisted herself into the sheltered, cavelike interior, fumbled around for the large, flat rock at the back, and sat down, leaning against the wall, knees drawn up to her chest, hugging her legs.

She had no sense of time. Once in a while a car would pass, its headlights sweeping the rock beyond the overhang and going on by, and she was aware that she was here, that the surface beneath her was hard, that the wall at her back was cold and damp, and once in a while she changed position. But still she stayed and still she sat.

Far ahead, where she could see a piece of sky, she saw clouds moving across the moon; the breeze picked up—she could hear it rustling the bushes outside—but it didn't touch her here. If she was cold, she didn't feel it. She was alone, that much she knew—possibly more alone than she had ever been in her life. But in her aloneness, she felt as though she were seeing things more clearly than she had ever seen them before.

It all had to do with self-liking. That's where it all began. Not the same as being selfish; not the same as being self-centered. It had to do simply with having something that nobody could take away from her, not ever—not even the Stephanie Kings of the world—and that was the feeling that she had value, she was important, she was worthwhile. Worth more than the monthly payments on a truck. Worth more than a shared bed over at the Prathers' house. Worth more than a ring to wear to school to show around in gym class.

For reasons she did not know, her parents wanted her to marry Harless. For reasons she could not begin to understand, they wanted that even more than they would like her to finish high school, which neither of them had done. She believed that Harless loved her. She believed that her mother did, too.

She couldn't believe anything about her father. Ray Herndon, Mystery Man. But this no longer mattered. What mattered now was what she felt about herself.

"Elizabeth Pearl," she said at last, as she climbed down off the rock, brushing the damp earth off the back of her jeans and jacket. "There's nobody else who's ever going to look after you as well as yourself." And she started home.

She could tell by the light in the sky that time had passed, but she had no watch. Just that peculiar shade of gray coming up over the horizon, like milk mixed into darkness, which meant the night was changing.

The bulb still burned on the porch, and as soon as Beth got inside, she turned it off. When she started across the floor, however, she noticed light coming from the kitchen around the corner, and then she saw her mother sitting at the dinette table in her robe, her father standing in the hallway in his pajamas.

She blinked. "Why you waiting up?"

Ray Herndon's voice was soft so as not to wake Lyle there on the couch, but it did not disguise his fury. "You know what time it is, girl?"

"No . . ."

"Well, take a look."

Beth glanced toward the little white clock near the TV. Four-twenty.

"I didn't know it was so late."

"Where in the world have you been?" That was Mother. She was not looking at Beth's face, but rather her clothes, and as Beth looked down, she noticed the dirt on her jeans and the sleeves of her jacket—the burrs that had stuck to the sides of her pants.

"Maybe I got to change my mind about Harless, but I never thought he'd keep you out all night," said Ray.

"He didn't. He brought me home hours ago."

"Then who *were* you with?" Mother demanded.

"Nobody. I was by myself."

They stared at her unbelieving. Beth stood rigidly in the center of the room, wishing they would invite her to sit down, wishing they could all sit there at the table together and just talk. She knew how foolish that would sound, were she even to suggest it, with her dad going off to work in a little more than two hours, her mother going to Goffs' at eight. They needed their sleep, and they'd already been waiting she didn't know how long.

Mother's face was contorted with anger or disappointment, Beth didn't know which, and her nose was red. "Didn't we try our best to bring you up right? Didn't we tell you right from wrong?" Lorna said.

"Right from wrong what?" Beth asked. "What do you think I've been doing?"

On the couch, Lyle stirred, raised his head and squinted, then plopped back down again.

"Elizabeth Pearl, you go out with a grown man and come home at four-thirty in the morning with dirt on your back, what do you expect us to think?"

"I was alone, Ma. I walked up the road to the cave," Beth told her, going a few steps closer, and she felt a strange sense of courage now, a sureness about herself that amazed her.

194

Even if her dad took the belt to her, it wouldn't change what she was or what she could be. "I was up there trying to figure things out—trying to figure what I'm supposed to think when I find out my dad promised to help Harless Prather with his truck payments if he would take me off your hands. Is that what you want? Me to run off with Harless? That thought's enough to keep anybody occupied till four in the morning."

Neither of her parents moved. Her father's face seemed gray.

"Beth, what in the world are you talkin' about?" said her mother. "You're not near old enough to marry."

"That's what I thought, too," Beth said, still looking at her father.

Ray's mouth worked a moment or two before he found the words to speak: "You talk like I'm payin' someone to take you away."

"Well, that's the way my ears heard it. Why didn't you just tie me in a sack when I was born, Dad—drop me in the river—you so anxious to be rid of me?"

"Beth . . . !" Mother's voice had a tremor in it.

But it was her father who took the floor now. "You listen to me, Beth." His eyes were earnest, not angry. "It's no secret I like Harless. Like him better than most boys I seen around here. It's no secret either I'd be happy if the two of you was to marry by and by. And when it come to me finally that he was liking you in that way, hinting at marrying, wondering how he could afford it, I said I'd help out on his truck payments—like a father-in-law. I never said it till I knew he was that sweet on you. I swear to God. There's no price in all the world high enough to buy you away from me." He stopped, and Beth heard him swallow.

The words were like an arm that had settled around her shoulder before she even realized it was there, like warmth seeping through her skin, her muscles, and on into her blood-stream. She was afraid to ask all the questions that swam in her head for fear it would break the spell. If ever she wanted to carry something with her the rest of her life, it was what her father had just said. It didn't make sense, but those were his words and they came from his mouth.

And so she told him right out: "If that's true, Dad, it's the nicest thing I ever heard from you, and I don't want to ruin it. I guess maybe I'd better get to bed."

Their eyes met. For a moment it seemed that Ray Herndon didn't want to end things there. But no one had slept, they all were tired, and when he let her go with a nod, Beth walked on down the hall.

She entered the bedroom quietly, took off her clothes, and fumbled about in the dresser drawer for her pajamas. But when she had gently crawled in under the covers, being careful not to wake her sister, Geraldine said, "Should've been me they were chewing on, not you."

"I didn't know you were awake," Beth whispered. "You just get home, too? How long have they been up waiting?"

"No, I've been home for hours. But they've been up a good long while. Where'd you go, Beth?"

"Up to the rocks—the cave. Just wanted to think things out."

"About Harless?"

"Partly."

"You going to marry him?"

"I don't know, Gerry."

Beth settled down on her pillow, pulling the covers up under her chin, wanting to remember what her father had said, word for word, the way he had said it, the look on his face. . . . If that wasn't love for her, what was?

Geraldine turned over, taking some of the covers with her. And then Beth heard her sob.

She lifted her head and listened again. "Gerry?"

On the far side of the bed, Gerry was rooting down under the blanket, the sobs muffled but coming faster. Beth slid down, pulled the covers up over her head, making a tent for themselves, and put one hand on Geraldine's shoulder. "Gerry? Tell me. What's wrong?"

Geraldine rolled over and pressed her face against Beth's arm, holding it there. Hot tears spilled out against Beth's skin.

"*Tell* me!" Beth whispered again.

"It's . . . it's me that's going to have a baby this time," Gerry told her. "Jack Carey's child."

10

How, Beth wondered, would this roller coaster of a night ever end? It seemed only a few hours ago that she had stood at the bathroom mirror, telling herself she was beautiful. Then her father's cutting comments about her looks, her half-nakedness in the truck with Harless, her words with Harless, her night in the cave, her father's strange remark about her worth, which she would remember always, and now, another sad blessing.

"Gerry . . ." It was all she could manage to say as she groped for something more helpful. "You sure about this now?"

Geraldine was breathing through her mouth, her nose clogged. "Missed two periods. Threw up once at school, and feel like I'm going to even when I don't. What other signs are there?"

The blind leading the blind. Beth hadn't the slightest idea. In the darkness beneath the blanket, she reached over and stroked the side of Geraldine's face, warm and wet to the touch. "Gerry," she asked finally, "didn't you know this could happen?"

"I thought of it, but Jack said I couldn't get pregnant unless we did it every week. Only times we did it was when he got his brother's car." She sniffled again. "I figured that . . . me being fourteen, well . . ." Then she was crying again, and her words came out in angry little squeaks: "Dad and Ma do it all the time, Beth, and there's still a year or two between babies."

"I wished you'd talked to me, Gerry. Talked to someone, anyway. Not that I'd have had the answers. . . ." Beth sighed. "Those encyclopedias sure wouldn't have helped. I already looked." She was trying, lamely, to make a joke. Then, "Does Jack know?"

"He knows I've been throwing up. Acts like he's mad at me or something. Said he was going to try to get me one of those pregnancy tests at the drugstore you take yourself, but he hasn't. Costs ten dollars." She rolled over on her back, and Beth could feel her holding the covers up away from her face with one hand. "Beth," she said desperately, "I'm only *fourteen*!"

Beth swallowed. And she was only fifteen. A few more weeks in the truck with Harless and it could have been her. She'd needed love that badly.

Harless, however, would have been glad. Harless would have waltzed her off to get married, made a place for her in his parents' house, raised the child proudly. She didn't want that yet, however. Wasn't sure what she wanted. What she did know this night was that she was strong again, stronger than she'd thought. Knew that her father loved her, maybe, and that even if he didn't, she cared about herself. But who would care for Gerry?

"When are you going to tell Ma?" Beth asked gently.

"Oh, Lord, Beth, I can't."

"Gerry, it's going to show!"

"Dad'll take the belt to me."

"Not with a baby in you, he won't. If you've been pregnant since February, you'll be due in . . ." Beth pressed her fingers one at a time against the mattress, counting off the months. "October. By then, everyone at school will . . ." She stopped.

"Only good part about this whole thing is that I don't have to go back to school in the fall," Gerry said.

An engulfing sadness seemed to swallow Beth up—sadness not for herself but for the rest of the family. All the children coming along next—Ruth Marie, Betty Jo, Shirley, and the boys—what kind of model would there be for them?

Beth drew her knees up and rested one arm around Gerry's waist. "Jack say anything about marrying?"

Gerry gave a bitter laugh. "Jack Carey would be the last boy I can think of who'd want to marry. And I'm not so sure I'd want to spend a solid month looking at him, much less the rest of my life."

"Gerry, I thought you liked him. You *must* have liked him to . . ."

"I liked him because I thought he really cared about me, you know? I mean, he was always saying how he could hardly get through a week without me; how he needed my k-kisses. Well, now he gets along real well without them. Sees me coming down the hall at school and turns the other way."

"What are you going to do?"

"I don't know. In gym I did all kinds of handsprings. Stood on my head and jumped the trampoline. Even bought myself some Ex-Lax and took half the box. Made me so sick I thought I was going to die, but nothing happened."

"Well, no matter what, you know I love you."

Geraldine turned toward her and buried her head on Beth's shoulder.

April passed quietly in the Herndon household. Wild rhododendron blossomed high on the rocky ledge behind their trailer, redbud trees opened their lavender blooms, and the new green of the hill behind Crandall was dotted here and there with white and yellow as each day the sun rose a bit higher in the sky.

The turkey vulture would wait until the sun had been up for some time, burning off the morning mist from the river and drying out his dew-covered wings. Then he would soar out over the river on the heated currents of air, and Beth would often see the shallow V-shape of his huge wings as they caught the rising updrafts.

Ray and Lorna spoke politely, softly, to Beth, and because they were concerned about her—concerned, too, that Harless had not come by for two and a half weeks—the distress signals in Geraldine went unnoticed.

Beth was up to the *P*s now in the business dictionary, but

doubted she would finish the book before the end of the semester. Her aim was to at least make it through the *T*s. The dedication that she had given all her subjects did not go unnoticed. Mr. Emerson commented on it in biology. In English, Beth concentrated on her theme papers, going over each sentence and paragraph, looking for ways they could be improved. It was tedious, but she needed to test herself, to see if it could be done. The day she received a paper back with a *B*+ instead of a *C*−, she carried it home proudly in her notebook but did not brag. Did not even show it to her parents.

Things were different between Beth and her father. As far as she could tell, it was simply his statement that there wasn't enough money in the world for anyone to buy her away from him, and her response that it was the nicest thing he'd ever said. What it was, in effect, was a declaration of love on both sides, though not exactly in those words.

Why they couldn't have done this before, she didn't know. It did not explain his faultfinding in the past; made no guarantees for the future. But it had opened a window between them through which each saw the other in a new light, and for the time being, that window was enough for Beth. If good grades upset him for whatever reason—*her* good grades, no one else's—she would keep them to herself.

It was hard to get help for her spelling from her family. Gerry stayed to herself, Mother had work of her own to do, and now Ruth Marie was busy teaching Betty Jo and Bud to make May baskets, which, she said, they were supposed to fill with flowers and leave on people's doorsteps early the morning of May first.

Ray Herndon did not mention Harless. He mercifully brought home no stories of what Harless had done or said as he made his deliveries. Mother, too, kept her questions to herself, but Beth could feel their eyes on her as she moved from room to room.

Beth managed to keep a tight hold on fourth place in the daily typing tests, and she took comfort in that—that and Miss Talbot's quiet confidence in her. What she did not take comfort in were Clarice's questions about Harless at lunchtime.

"You still going with him, Beth?" she asked outright one day.

Beth, who had been listening to the 11:46 go through on its way to New York, had not even heard the question. She was thinking how everybody on that train had not only a place to leave *from* but a place to go *to*. Somebody waiting for him, maybe. Thinking about Miss Talbot catching the evening train to Chicago or the morning train to New York. Beth herself could get on that train some morning and be in New York, she'd heard, by ten-thirty at night. Didn't have to go to an airport to leave West Virginia. Just hitch a ride into Crandall with her suitcase, climb onto that train, and disappear off the face of the earth. Start up a whole new life somewhere else. If she wanted.

"Are you?" Clarice's voice again.

"What?"

"You and Harless. What's happened?"

Beth lowered herself slowly back to earth. "Why are you so eager to know? You want him?"

Clarice gave her a look. "You ever drop him, Joan might

be interested. She was at the movies the other night, and when she came out, she said that the skinny boy with the orange hair was talking to some girls on the sidewalk. Didn't know if he was with any of them or not."

"He's got a right to talk to folks," Beth said, and then, "I'm having a hard time making up my mind about things, Clarice, that's all."

Her friend studied her. "'Things' could be anything at all, Beth."

"Him and me, then. What I want to do when I graduate. I want to have something I'm good at. Don't want to get myself cornered."

"Oh." Clarice drank the last of her milk, then set the carton down. "Well, I'm thinking about lab technician, myself. I'll major in it, but I figure if my dad studied to be a detective and ended up a dentist, anything at all could happen. Sometimes life sort of takes care of itself."

Beth smiled. "Sometimes, maybe. What's with you and Johnny Stone? I thought you'd been going out."

Clarice grinned. "We have. That's why I'm not interested in Harless."

Beth came home on her birthday to find cutouts of birthday cakes on the windows and a big SWEET SIXTEEN sign on the door. She figured Ruth Marie had made them in advance, waited until Beth had left for school that morning, then hastily put them up before her own bus came. She smiled to herself. What *did* girls do without sisters?

Shirley and Douglas were at the door waiting for her,

yelping their birthday greetings and talking about the cake they had helped bake. Lorna herself was in the kitchen, frantically spreading the last of the Pillsbury Chocolate Fudge frosting.

"Thought I could get this done before you got home," she said.

"Glad you didn't," Beth told her. "I get to scrape the bowl." She shared the frosting with Shirley and Douglas.

Gerry was sick at supper and did not come to the table, but the others enjoyed the spaghetti Mother had made, and when the cake came out, and then the presents—a sample bottle of shampoo, a box of Brach's chocolate-covered raisins, a lipstick, a polyester top—Beth opened them slowly, commenting on each in turn, trying to make this moment happy for all of them, knowing that Gerry's secret back in the bedroom would rain down on their heads soon enough.

"Kisses all around!" she said, jumping up and kissing Mother first. She went around the room, and Lyle, of course ducked. Bud screeched and gagged, but Douglas contributed a hug as well. In all the laughter, the knock at the door went unnoticed until it was repeated again still louder. Shirley ran to answer and there was Harless.

The younger children greeted him as though he'd never stopped coming by, hung onto his arm, tried to climb up his back. He swatted them off with his usual good humor, glancing once or twice in Beth's direction.

"You're just in time for some birthday cake," Lorna said, getting up for a clean saucer. "Come on in here, Harless, and sit down."

"Whose birthday?" Harless asked, and Beth couldn't tell whether or not he was joking.

"Beth's!" yelled Douglas. "She's sixty years!"

The house rocked with laughter.

"Well, here's to the old woman then," Harless said, raising an imaginary glass. Beth smiled.

They talked about Wheelers' Bakery while Harless ate, talked about the potholes that had developed in the roads over the winter and had not yet been repaired. Talked all around Beth, in fact, without mentioning her name. But finally Harless put his fork down and said, "Well, now that Beth's sixteen, thought I'd come by and give her a driving lesson."

"Your truck or mine?" Ray quipped, and that brought a laugh.

"I'll risk it," said Harless. He looked at Beth. "Want to go?"

"Sure."

"Won't need a jacket. Warm as toast out there."

She walked on out to the truck with him and giggled as he put her in the driver's seat this time. The whole family came to the door to watch and hooted loudly as Beth started, then killed, the engine.

"Head for the falls, not civilization," Harless told her. "Folks see you at the wheel, they'll be running off the road, going every which way."

"Don't make me laugh, Harless. I've got to mind what I'm doing," she told him.

She knew what to do, having watched her father and Harless drive so often, but it was her coordination that gave her problems. When to brake and when to shift and when to disengage the clutch were all unfamiliar rhythms that she hoped, like the typewriter, she would get the hang of directly. She pulled jerkily into the parking lot at the falls, and the truck lurched forward in a series of jolts before the engine died. They sat there a moment, laughing.

"How've you been?" Harless asked her.

"Been okay. Busy."

"School going all right and everything?"

"Yes. Lots of work to do the closer we get to vacation."

It seemed awkward sitting there in the truck making small talk. This was the very seat where Harless had held her, stroked her, where they had each undressed to the waist. This was the place—the only place, perhaps—where Beth had felt for sure that she was loved. She'd given it up for what? She wondered if it was a mistake to have come here again tonight, starting the questions all over again.

"I've been going out some," Harless confessed at last.

"So I've heard."

"Word sure gets around. Can't sneeze your neighbor don't bless you."

Beth smiled.

Harless fidgeted a little on his side of the seat. "Just wanted to find out if I'd miss you, is what," he told her.

"Did you? Miss me, I mean?"

"Not much. Not when I'm asleep, anyways." He reached over and took her hand without looking at her. "You been going out?"

"Went out the night you left me off. I didn't get home until four in the morning." She stole him a look but Harless

207

was staring straight ahead, and his hand stopped stroking her thumb. "I walked on up to that cave off the road a ways and sat in there having myself a good think," she continued. His hand seemed to grow warm again over hers.

"Must have got a good lot of thinking in," he said.

"What I decided, Harless, was that I can't be good at anything unless I feel good about myself. You know what I mean?"

"I'm not sure."

"Making plans for myself. If I don't have enough love for me, then I don't have any extra to give. I don't want to marry till I've got enough good feelings there's some to spare."

Harless was quiet for some time. "You have anyone else in mind?" he asked finally.

"No."

"Willing to set a date, then?"

"Not yet, Harless. You wait till I get out of school and work a year, then you ask me again if you still want to."

"I maybe could meet someone else by then."

"I expect you could."

"Or *you* could meet someone."

"That could happen, too." Lordy, was this Beth Herndon talking? Was she all that sure of herself?

"And you're willing to take that chance?" Harless asked.

"Seems like a bigger chance going into marriage before I'm ready. And coming out here to the falls like we were doing was sure pushing me toward it." She thought again of Gerry. Thought of telling Harless, even, but knew it wasn't her secret to tell. "I still love you," she said. "I never loved any other boy before. That's why, if you marry me—if it works out that we do—I want you to be getting someone who thinks something of herself. Won't take her feelings out on you."

Harless sighed. "Figured you'd say something like that."

"What do *you* want, Harless? All this while I'm working on myself, what'll be going on with you?"

"I just don't spend too much of my life troubling myself about it," he said. "I take what comes. That's the way I am, Beth. I want a wife and children, a job and a house, and a good truck to carry me around. Beyond that I don't see the point in worry. I see a chance, I take it. If not, well . . ." He shrugged.

She thought he was angry then, but instead, he reached under the seat and pulled out a small box. "Anyway, got you a present."

"Didn't think you even knew it was my birthday."

"Knew it was coming up, so I asked your dad which day."

Beth untied the ribbon and opened the lid. Under a square of cotton she found a silver-plated charm bracelet, with three little silver charms already attached to it: a typewriter, a truck, and a house.

"Oh, Harless!" She fingered it lovingly.

He reached over and turned the typewriter around for her to see the keys. "That's what you'll be thinking on for the next few years," he told her, and then, pointing to the truck, "That's what I'll be thinking on. And the house? Well, I guess we'll both have to wait and see on that one."

His face was close to hers now, and Beth reached up and

209

kissed him, one hand on the back of his neck. That wonderful smell of his skin . . .

"Well, I'd better get you back; you've got school tomorrow," he said. "You want to drive or me?"

"You can stand to risk your life one more time, I'd like to try it," she said.

When Beth entered the trailer later, her father was watching wrestling on TV with Bud and Lyle, and Ruth Marie and Betty Jo were doing the dishes. Beth went back to the bedroom to show Gerry her bracelet, but when she opened the door, Mother was sitting on the edge of the bed, Geraldine on the far side, propped against the wall, arms folded over her chest. Her nose was red, as though she'd been crying, but Lorna's face was ashen. Beth immediately turned to leave, but Gerry said, "Come on in, Beth."

Beth came. She sat at the foot of the bed.

"You know what this girl just told me, Beth?" asked Lorna.

Beth looked at Gerry. "I think so."

"How long you know this?"

"Not too long."

"And didn't tell me?"

"I figured it wasn't mine to tell, Ma. You'd find out soon enough."

"Oh, that I did." Lorna closed her eyes for a moment, lips pressed tightly together. She tried a time or two to speak, but the corners of her mouth sagged, and she struggled to keep from crying. At last she asked simply, "Where did I go wrong, Beth? What didn't I do for you girls I should have done?"

Beth felt a momentary rush of anger. What right had her mother to express disappointment? Surprise, even? Should she tell her how it was a matter of too little information too late? She remembered when Mother had come into her and Gerry's room four years ago and placed a box of Kotex on their dresser.

"This here's for when you need it," she had said, "which is I expect any day now. You let me know when you want more, hear?" But that was a month after Beth had started her periods and had already been folding up toilet paper and lining her pants. The truth was, she discovered then, daughters don't open up to mothers who don't open up themselves. They ask other girls or maybe the nurse at school.

But it wasn't as simple as just knowing facts. She could imagine that no matter how much she might have known about life, if she'd needed love badly enough, she might still have had sex with Harless in his truck.

"Ma," she said, "maybe you did the best you could with Gerry and me. It's what you can do for Ruth Marie and Betty Jo and Shirley that matters now."

She didn't realize how heartless that would sound until she saw that Gerry was crying again. Why was she being called upon to play the mother role, anyway? Anger stabbed at her again. It was Lorna who should have been knowing the right things to say, Lorna doing the comforting, not she.

Mother dabbed at her own eyes. "One minute I'm celebrating my oldest child's birthday, and then I come in to see how Gerry's doing and find out I got a grandchild on the way." She looked over at Geraldine and slowly shook her head. "Honey, you're as green as I was when I was a bride, but I didn't think it would catch up with you so fast. For that I'm truly sorry. Thought I had plenty of time to tell you what you should know."

"Well, I can't think of a time I *didn't* have questions," Gerry said bitterly, "so the sooner you start talking to Ruth Marie, the better."

Lorna bit her lip. "Jack going to marry you?"

"I'm not going to marry him, Ma."

Mother's hands dropped to her lap. "What are you telling me, Geraldine Louise?"

"I'm saying I've got to have this baby without his daddy, because Jack Carey would make about the worst husband in the world, unless he grows up fast the next six months or so, which I doubt very much."

"We going to raise this child on our own?"

"Ma, what else is there to do?"

Lorna looked at Gerry a good long time, then turned to Beth. "You think maybe this could be a blessing in disguise? Maybe the good Lord sent this one to take the place of the one I lost? Never figured it could happen that way, but now that I think on it . . ."

"No, Ma," Beth said. "I don't think God rains down babies or takes them away, either one."

"Well, maybe so. Part of me wants to grab you by the shoulders, Geraldine, and shake the daylights out of you, and the other part of me already wants to hold that child. We'll just have to make room." She leaned awkwardly across the bed with her arms out, Gerry leaned forward, and they hugged.

Gerry went to school each morning with Lyle, and it was agreed that she should finish out the ninth grade. Father knew about it now; Beth could tell because of his silence around Gerry. Not a hostile silence, just a sad sort of disbelief and disappointment, too sharp to put into words. Nor was there any more mention of Beth's leaving school and going to work in the diner, now that her sixteenth birthday was past.

It was Wednesday of the following week when, as Beth walked into typing class, one of the girls turned and said, "Congratulations!"

Beth's first thought was that she had found out about Gerry and was cruelly rubbing it in. But the smile was genuine, and Beth wondered if the girl meant her birthday the week before.

"What for?" she asked. Some of the boys were smiling, too.

"Haven't you heard?" one of them said.

"No. What?"

"You and Stephanie King? Don't you read the announcements?"

"What?"

"Go look on the bulletin board."

Beth put her books on her desk and tried to imagine what they were talking about. Stephanie King had held top place in typing all semester, so that wasn't news, and Beth couldn't be more than fourth place herself—third at the most. Yes, maybe she was third, but that wasn't anything to congratulate her for.

She scanned the notices—the job announcements and the scholarship applications, even the list of students who had made the honor roll the last grading period. She wasn't one of them and never had been.

And then her eye caught a yellow sheet of paper in one corner. *The Talbot-Wentworth Duo Award,* it said. Beth stared at the word *duo.* It wasn't any of the words in her business dictionary. She read on:

Susan Talbot and Martha Wentworth are pleased to announce the recipients of their new Duo Award, which provides all expenses for two students to attend a three-week intensive study seminar on the campus of West Virginia University in Morgantown.

This program, sponsored by a number of high schools throughout the state, provides selected students an intensive period of study and exploration in the fields of their choice, as well as consultation with experts who will help each student in his or her career planning.

One student is chosen for the Duo Award based upon superior academic performance, and this year's selection is Stephanie King. The other student is chosen on the basis of progress and motivation, and this honor goes to Beth Herndon. . . .

"So you've already heard the news!" It was Miss Talbot, who had just come in.

Beth was speechless. She hadn't even known that there was such an award. Hadn't *wanted* to know. When other students talked about awards and scholarships, she always tuned them out, never once believing that such a prize could come to her. But to have to go anywhere—even to the bathroom—with Stephanie King, to have to talk with her, sit with her, when for months now, they'd been avoiding each other's eyes . . .

"I can't believe it," Beth said aloud.

"Me, either." It was Stephanie's voice somewhere behind her.

"Nice things *do* happen sometimes," Miss Talbot said, smiling. "Take your seats, class, but you can congratulate our winners if you like."

The other students clapped, and Miss Talbot sat on the edge of her desk in her beige slacks and bright coral blouse and told about the program at Morgantown the last three weeks of June. Other students would be selected to go from Crandall High, of course, but at their own expense, and this year she and Miss Wentworth had decided to each sponsor a student in their Duo Award. Students could select four different courses to study. There would be stenography, chemistry, business, computers, creative writing, music, art . . . whatever they liked. There were no grades, no credits. They learned because they wanted to.

"Miss Wentworth has the papers for your parents to sign," Miss Talbot said, looking at Beth and Stephanie. "She'll give them to you later in the day. But meanwhile, girls, congratulations again."

By lunchtime, a lot of people had heard the news, and people kept coming up to Beth in the hall, offering congratulations. And because she was walking around with a perpetual smile on her face, boys she scarcely knew smiled back. Her joy was contagious. Stephanie, of course, did not come near Beth, and Beth said nothing to her. The awkwardness of it grew worse as the day wore on. Not even Clarice guessed the depth of their dislike for each other.

"I wish it was me going with you," Clarice said, however, at lunch. "Wouldn't it be *fun*, the two of us in the dorm? Talbot's right, though. Stephanie certainly has the grades, and you've moved up faster than anybody else in typing this semester. You're going to have more fun in Morgantown! I'll bet you'll meet some fantastic boys. Harless will be jealous as anything."

Beth only smiled. She wasn't going because it might make Harless jealous. She was doing this for herself. Even if it meant sleeping in the same room with Stephanie King.

She and Stephanie were not in the same English class, so when Miss Wentworth congratulated Beth later, she congratulated her alone.

"Both Miss Talbot and I have been so pleased with your progress this semester, Beth," she said. "I've heard it from other teachers, too. Your spelling is better, your grammar . . . I've seen a real improvement in your papers. I know English isn't one of your favorite subjects, but that's not important. It's what kind of a try you give it."

She reached one beautifully manicured hand into a drawer for some papers, pointing out to Beth where her parents were to sign. "Everything's provided," she said. "All you have to bring are your clothes."

"I'm really looking forward to it," Beth said, a smile taking over her face. "Farthest I've ever been is Hawk's Nest."

"You sound like me when I was sixteen," Miss Wentworth said. "Only trips I'd ever taken were back and forth between Huntington and Charleston. But there was a college teacher who lived up the street from us, and somehow she took an interest in me—gave me books to read and helped me apply for a scholarship to Marshall University. I got it, I graduated, and here I am."

"But you could teach anywhere. New York, even!"

Miss Wentworth laughed. "I thought of it once—Boston, actually, not New York. But then I decided this was payback time." She locked her hands behind her head and smiled at Beth. "Payback time for a lot of us—for Miss Talbot, too. We'd like to give other students the chance that someone gave us. And that's awfully satisfying, Beth. It's hard to explain. But it's better than Boston. Of that I'm sure."

When Beth got on the bus that afternoon, the seat behind Mrs. Shayhan was taken, so she moved farther back and slid in next to the window, imagining herself bursting into the trailer when she got home and announcing the news. She turned when she felt someone sit down on the seat beside her, and then she discovered that it was Stephanie King.

"Congratulations," Stephanie said.

"Yeah. You, too," said Beth. She could see out of the corner of her eye the way Stephanie was toying with a paper clip and sensed how uncomfortable she was. It had taken courage to sit down beside her, that was certain.

"I called Mom over the lunch hour to tell her the news," said Stephanie, "and she said she could drive us up to Morgantown next month. I wondered if you'd like to go with us. I think the program starts on a Monday."

Beth tried desperately to think of an excuse. Dad couldn't drive her up on a Monday, he'd be working. So would Harless. And then she thought, Elizabeth Pearl, are you going to go all your life mad at a girl who maybe could teach you something?

"Sure," she said. "I guess I'll need a ride up there, since Dad will be working."

"It'll probably be early in the morning; registration's at noon. I'll let you know."

There was more silence for a time. Then Stephanie added, "Did you see that list of things we're not supposed to bring with us? No stereos, no skateboards, no furniture, no hot plates . . . Can you imagine who would bring any of that for just three weeks?"

Beth chuckled a little, too. Not that she had a stereo to bring, of course. "I heard we can wear shorts if it gets hot," she offered.

"And they have really great picnics on weekends," said Stephanie.

So finally they were talking. Cautiously, at first, then a bit more relaxed. Beth wondered if they would ever discuss that Christmas basket. Sometime, maybe, when they were feeling a whole lot different about each other.

"Beth?" came Mrs. Shayhan's voice, and Beth realized that the bus had not only stopped at her home, but had actually gone all the way to the falls and back. This was her last chance to get off.

She and Stephanie laughed as Beth stood up and walked to the door.

Since she was late getting home, she found Ruth Marie, Betty Jo, and Bud already there, horsing around outside. Mrs.

Maxwell flagged her down as she started up the steps, and Beth went over.

"I got Shirley and Douglas," the small woman said. "Gerry was sick, so your ma made an appointment at the clinic and Mrs. Goff drove them into Crandall."

"Oh," Beth said. "You want me to take the kids then?"

"Wouldn't complain one bit if you did." The woman laughed good-naturedly.

In Mrs. Maxwell's cramped living room, Shirley and Douglas were playing a game of standing over an empty fruit jar, seeing who could drop the most clothespins inside it. Mrs. Maxwell shuffled about, collecting their things.

"How's the romance going with that Prather boy?" She smiled over at Beth. "He going to be the one?"

Beth smiled back. "Wish I knew."

"I tell you what to do then." Mrs. Maxwell nodded emphatically. "Boil you an egg, cut it in half, and throw out the yolk. Then fill up the center with salt, and that's what you have for your dinner. Don't drink a drop of anything, but go straight to bed, and in your dream, the man you're going to marry will bring you some water. You'll see him clear as glass."

Beth laughed. "I'll be so thirsty I'll just grab the cup and forget all about the man."

"You try it now," the old woman said. "My mama said it worked for her."

"Did you ever try it?"

"Naw. I knew before I was thirteen years old who I'd marry, and it looks like I did."

219

Beth was still smiling as she took the two younger children home and had just made them a snack in front of the TV when her father came in, beating the junior-high bus this time.

Beth could hardly wait to tell him about the course at Morgantown, but she couldn't just shove the papers at him before he'd hardly sat down. She waited until he was seated at the dinette table with a soft drink, shirt sleeves rolled up, before she walked over, grinning.

He gave a little smile. "Look like the cat that swallowed the canary," he told her.

"I am!" Beth grinned even more broadly and pulled the papers out from behind her. "Look!" She thrust them in his hands. The one on top was the same announcement that was on the bulletin board in typing class.

"What is it?"

"Read it! You'll see!"

"Where's Lorna?"

Beth sighed with impatience. "She took Gerry to the clinic for a checkup or something; Mrs. Goff drove them. Come on, Dad. It's something nice! You've got to sign it, anyway."

"Why don't you just tell me, girl, and save my eyes. They've been hurting me some."

Beth smiled reproachfully and pointed to the paragraph that told how she had been chosen for her progress and motivation. "Just read this one paragraph, Dad. It's something wonderful."

He looked where she was pointing. Any minute now, Beth thought, he'd see her name, and then he'd want to read the rest. She'd see his face break into that little grin and watch it take over his whole face. She waited, grinning herself.

But suddenly her father got up from the table and took his soft drink to the kitchen, leaving the papers behind. "Well, you don't want to tell me, then don't, but I don't have time to play games. Got work to do." His face was a strange color of pink. And without another glance in her direction, Ray put his drink in the refrigerator, then went out the back door and began rummaging about the junk pile, sorting through sheets of aluminum and plywood.

Beth stood numbly by the window, incredulous. What had she possibly done now to make him angry? Just when she thought things were going better between them! It wasn't as though he had to use his eyes all day. All he did was stand at the grill waiting for the counter girls to call out orders. . . . His feet might be tired, but not his eyes.

She stared at the man whose face was still that peculiar shade of pink. And then, like the current rushing down the New River, encircling the rocks at the falls, a certainty swept over her. "Oh, my God," she whispered. "He can't read."

She sucked in her breath. Was it possible? No, it couldn't be! Sometime, *some*time, she must have seen him reading. The newspaper? They didn't take a newspaper. Books? Magazines? She'd never seen him reading any. And then, like a slide show, other pictures came to mind: her mother doing the income tax each year; her mother reading picture books to the younger children while her father made up his own stories; Mother singing in church while Dad sang only the verses he'd memorized and silently held the hymnbook for the others; Dad refusing to help her with her spelling; Dad never looking at her report card . . . No, he wasn't angry with her; perhaps he never had been. He was embarrassed.

Dear Lord Jesus and God, she prayed, *we've been a family full of secrets.*

How hard it must have been for him and Mother to keep it to themselves. Month after month, year after year—here at home, in the diner—the excuses, the embarrassment. . . . Mother had probably even gone with him to take his driving test, to read the questions. All these years she had been covering up for him to save his self-esteem. Did he even know he could get help? Beth wondered. Probably not. Oh, Dad, she thought. I didn't mean to wring this out of you, but I'm glad I know.

Lyle's bus came and he slammed through the door and clumped on out to the kitchen for the Chee-Tos. "How come Gerry wasn't in school today?" he asked Beth.

Beth slowly stirred herself. "I leave before you do in the mornings," she reminded him. "I didn't even know Gerry was absent till Mrs. Maxwell told me."

The cellophane sack rustled as Lyle took a handful of Chee-Tos and dropped them into a bowl.

"What's wrong with her?" he asked, and when Beth didn't answer right away, he said, "Some of the kids are saying that Jack Carey knocked her up. That isn't true, is it?"

Beth turned. "Yes, Lyle, it is."

He whirled around and looked at her, then suddenly threw the bag down on the counter. "Some guy said Gerry was pregnant and I pasted him one. How come you didn't tell me?" he cried accusingly.

"How come you didn't tell Ma that Jack Carey didn't have a sister?" Beth asked, and when Lyle's face dropped, she said, "I didn't tell her, either, Lyle. My fault as much as it is yours."

Lyle stood motionless, too upset to eat. "She was seeing Jack Carey some of those nights she said she was baby-sitting. I knew that, too."

Beth's shoulders slumped as they looked at each other. "Well, there's no guarantee that even if we had told Ma, it would have changed things," she said at last. Lyle felt bad enough as it was.

"When is she going to have it?"

"October, I think." Beth studied him. "Lyle, we're not very good at talking in this family, but I'm going to ask you straight out: Do you know how babies are made?"

He stared at her aghast.

"I'm not asking you to tell me; just yes or no."

"I'm no dummy," he said.

"Well, Jack Carey was. He said that as long as they didn't do it every week, Gerry couldn't get pregnant. And Gerry figured that since she was only fourteen, it wouldn't happen to her. They were both wrong. All I'm saying is, if you ever even *think* about it . . ."

"You'd kill me," said Lyle.

"No, that's not what I meant. You go to someone who knows. Ask the school nurse. But you make sure you've got the facts right."

Somehow, Beth decided, she was going to get some booklets and leave them lying around. Stick them in the encyclopedias where *Sex* should be, maybe. And if Ma didn't tell Ruth Marie and Betty Jo pretty soon, she'd tell them herself; wasn't going to have them hear it secondhand from someone at school who didn't know any more than they did.

She tried to imagine herself walking in the health room at

school and asking Mrs. Lester for booklets about pregnancy. Imagined the nurse looking at her quizzically and saying, "Pregnancy, Beth?" "How babies get in, where they come out, and anything else there is to know," Beth would tell her, then laughed at the thought.

She opened four cans of beef stew and some creamed corn and had them simmering on the stove when Mrs. Goff's car pulled up. Gerry and Lorna got out. When they came inside, Gerry went back to the bedroom.

Lorna took off her flowered hat and set it on the shelf above the jackets. "Could wait your life away in the clinic!" she complained. "Could have put my fingers to use if I'd had something with me."

"What's wrong with Gerry?" Betty Jo wanted to know.

"What she's got, she'll get over," Mother said in reply, and went on out into the kitchen.

Beth went back to the bedroom. "Everything okay, Gerry?"

"I guess so. Doctor says so, anyway."

"You like him?"

"It's a her. Yeah, she's nice. Didn't give me a sermon, at least." She stretched out on the bed and stared up at the ceiling. "What am I going to do, Beth?"

"About what?"

"About everything."

"What do you want to do? What would you want to be doing if you weren't having this baby?"

"Just what I was doing before, I guess. Going out. Having fun." She shrugged. "I mean, what else *can* I do? I'm dumb, Beth. Always was, always will be."

224

"Listen, Gerry, everyone's smart at something."

"Yeah? Like what?"

"Like cooking or selling things in a shop. This baby isn't your whole life. A big part of it, but not everything."

Geraldine gave her a small smile. "Keep on saying nice things to me, Beth, because I'm going to need to hear a lot of them."

Supper was quiet. Lyle had turned the TV down low and nobody thought to turn it up again. While the three youngest sat on the couch with their plates in their laps, the others helped themselves to the stew and corn and passed a loaf of bread back and forth from dinette to card table.

"I got some news, Ma . . . Dad," Beth said at last.

"Well! She's finally going to tell us," said Ray, not looking up.

Beth only smiled. "I'm one of two girls picked to go to a three-week study course at the University in Morgantown in June, all expenses paid."

Lorna stopped eating and stared at her. "You get something in the mail, or what?"

"No, it was on the bulletin board at school. Miss Talbot and Miss Wentworth started a new award. Each year they're going to pick two students who they think are doing their best—one for her grades—that's Stephanie King—and the other for her progress, I guess it is. Her motivation, they said. And that's me."

Lorna still couldn't take it all in. "Where you going to stay in Morgantown?"

Beth told them about the dormitory, the courses of study, and how the program drew the best teachers from around the state. "It's like the Lord Jesus came down and said, 'Beth, what can I do for you?' and when I told him, he said, 'You got it; here it is,'" she added.

"How you going to get to Morgantown?" her father asked.

"I'll ride up with Stephanie King and her mother."

"Stephanie King!" said Gerry. "Isn't she the one who had that basket delivered here at Christmas?"

"Yep," said Beth. "And the first thing I'm going to learn from this course is how to get along with Stephanie King, if I have to choke to death learning."

"Well, Beth! I declare! That's some news, all right!" said her mother, smiling now. "My goodness, only two girls in the whole school picked!"

"More than that, but we're the only ones who get our way paid. Could hardly believe it myself," Beth said. But it was her father's reaction she wanted.

He reached for the salt; he reached for the pepper. He shook both over his stew and passed them on to Lyle. And then, when Beth thought surely he would withhold all comment whatever, he said softly, "You get up to Morgantown, Beth, maybe you won't want to come back."

She smiled at him then. "You'll just begin to enjoy the house without me, Dad, and here I'll be."

At six-thirty on the morning of June 12, Beth sat on a large rock across the road from the trailer, a nylon knapsack that Mother had bought at the Super Dollar at her feet. Stephanie and her mother weren't picking her up until six forty-five, but Beth had been ready so long that she could not contain her restlessness, so had come outside to wait, drinking in the early morning smell of wild honeysuckle, watching the sunlight catch the trees at the very top of the hill behind Crandall, then move slowly downward.

A fish leaped in the water—a smallmouth bass, she thought. Once she had sat so still on the bank she had seen a sunfish moving just below the surface. But she was too excited to sit still now. *Dear Lord Jesus and God,* she prayed, *I'm ready for anything you send me—except babies.*

She still wasn't sure how much God really had to do with things down here on Shadbush Road and how much He kept to Himself. Sometimes what people thought were blessings weren't that blessed at all, and sometimes the things that seemed about the worst that could happen made some kind of sense when you thought them over. Going to Morgantown, though, was a blessing, as far as she could see. She was grateful for it, wher*ever* it came from.

Beth thought again of her mother, and how Lorna called all her children blessings, even though each of them, in one way or another, had worn her down a little. Maybe Mother figured that should she and Dad need help themselves someday, the more children there were, the more they'd have to rely on. There was some kind of sense in that, Beth agreed. Sort of like the land itself. When the coal companies mined the land, they had to make it right again, had to put something back. Couldn't just do their strip-mining like they used to and walk off, leaving it ugly. And maybe that was Beth's job now—to take the best that West Virginia's teachers had to offer, to learn all she could, and then give something back.

She remembered what Lyle had said when Geraldine complained that she couldn't find *Charleston* in the encyclopedia. "'Cause nobody hardly ever heard of our state," Lyle had told her. How could anyone feel that way, with mountains all around them and the New River just across the road? Beth had wondered then. What could she do to make him feel different? she asked herself now.

She had said good-bye to Mother, who would be leaving the house in Geraldine's care now that vacation was here, and to Dad as he stood shaving in the bathroom. And in fifteen minutes or so, she would be starting a journey to a place she had never been, with a girl she hadn't thought she could like in a million years. Life was sure full of surprises.

Harless had come over the night before. He'd brought her a new charm for her bracelet, a tiny pair of silver eyeglasses. All that studying in Morgantown, he'd said, was going to wear her eyes out.

"Three weeks of studying," she'd told him, "isn't going to wear out anything but my backside."

When he'd left and she walked him out to his truck, he had kissed her, a long, slow kiss like he used to, and she thought about that from her perch on the rock.

Would he still be waiting for her when she came back from Morgantown? When she graduated from high school, two years off? After she'd worked for a year after that? She didn't know if it was fair to expect him to. One thing she did know, however: If Harless could love her, and if she liked herself, there were other boys, other men, who could love her, too.

The door of the trailer opened and Ray Herndon came out,

hands in his pockets. He waited while a van went by, then crossed the road and came over to the rock where Beth was sitting. He leaned against it, watching the road to the left where the Kings' car would be coming.

"You've been sitting out here awhile, honey. Figure she's late?"

"No, I'm early. Got ten minutes yet. I was just so excited I figured I'd wear out the floor pacing."

For a moment he didn't say anything. Shifted his feet once or twice, getting up his nerve, Beth thought, and she wondered what it was he wanted to tell her. To confess, finally, that he couldn't read? Since her discovery there in the house, Beth had not even asked her mother about it. She would sometime, but not now. A secret kept for sixteen years could go a few weeks longer.

But it wasn't that that Ray Herndon wanted to talk about.

"Beth," he said finally, "I been thinking some about how I've wronged you, and I . . . I just don't want you going off to Morgantown thinking I don't care."

She was almost afraid to look at him, afraid he wouldn't finish. She was still that thirsty for kindness. "About me, Dad?" Out of the corner of her eye, she saw him nod.

"'Bout the time you were twelve, I guess, starting junior high, and I seen you was a smart little thing, fight to get your way, I guess I worried that someday you might take it in your head to leave here. Leave Lorna and me. Go off somewhere to take a job. And the more I worried on it, the more I didn't think I could stand that—our family ending up like my own, maybe."

Beth listened, still as a wall.

"Don't know how I come to think like I did—never really sat down and planned it out—but seems to me, looking back, that I put you down ever' chance I got, trying to make you think you weren't so special, to keep you here, you see. Make you think you're lucky just to have a local boy look at you, treat you nice."

Beth closed her eyes and swallowed.

"But I see now—thinking about Gerry, too—I had that all wrong. If you stayed because you didn't think you'd amount to much, you wouldn't be the same Beth I loved all these years. You got to go where your heart tells you to go, girl, just like I did. If I'm lucky, you'll come back and see us now and then."

Had an idea ever been expressed so eloquently, Beth wondered, by a man who couldn't read?

"Dad," Beth said, "I've never been to Morgantown so I don't know what all it's got, but I don't think I'll be able to go to my window and see what I'm looking at right now—which is sunlight taking over that whole hill, piece by piece. Don't think I'll be able to step outside the dormitory and have me a river only a few yards off."

"There's other places in the world besides Morgantown," her father said. "Lots of places you haven't been, Beth."

They could see a blue car far off down the road, making its way slowly, like someone looking for the right house.

"The way I figure it," Beth said, "somebody gives me a chance like this, then I've got to give something, too. I can't promise where I'll be ten years from now, but if it's not

Crandall, I'll be back sure as spring. Sure as you see flowers on the shadbush."

The blue car came around the bend and began to slow down. Beth slid from the rock and picked up her bag.

"It's spring right now," her father said. "Be almost July before you're back."

"Till summer then," Beth told him, giving him a hug, and walked toward the car.